# KILLER IN OUR Pocket

## A DARK FFM ROMANCE

# Killer In Our Pocket

## A Dark FFM Romance

L. Clara

# CONTENTS

Listen it's a book about a hitman and a woman who is out for revenge for her sister who was abducted. Shit gets wild and chaotic. For a full list of triggers please see my website at https://lclaraauthor.com/

To all the people who have been told they're too much...this one's for you.

Ever wonder what a character's playlist would look like? Wonder no more.

Lunch – Billie Eilish

Cluster – Slipknot

Build a Bitch – Bella Poarch

Under Your Spell – Buffy the Vampire Slayer (Musical)

Crazy Bitch – Buckcherry

Cleanin' Out My Closet – Eminem

Killer Queen – Queen

Just A Girl – No Doubt

Killing In The Name – Rage Against The Machine

Torn To Pieces – Pop Evil

Another One Bites The Dust – Queen

Snuff – Slipknot

Cluster – Slipknot

Tattered & Torn – Slipknot

How to Save a Life – The Fray

Chasing Cars – Snow Patrol

a thousand years – Christina Perri

That's My Girl – Russ

Creep – Radiohead

Heart-Shaped Box – Nirvana

Highway to Hell – AC/DC

I've Got a Theory – Buffy the Vampire Slayer (Musical)

Under Your Spell – Buffy the Vampire Slayer (Musical)

Firework – Katy Perry

Burn – Ellie Goulding

Fire With Fire – FEMME

I Kissed A Girl – Katy Perry

Free Fallin' – Tom Petty

Broken – Seether, Amy Lee

Dog Days Are Over – Florence + The Machine

Last Kiss – Pearl Jam

Twelve Years ago

I wake up to screams echoing throughout the house. Bolting out of bed, I run out of my room to find Mom screaming and sobbing at the door to my sister's room.

"Mom? What's wrong?" Tears threaten to fall as the fear of what I'm going to find builds the closer I creep closer toward Ivy's room.

My mom doesn't acknowledge me. The screams only seem to grow louder the closer I get. Once I reach the door, I see Dad is sitting on Ivy's bed. His head in his hands, shaking uncontrollably.

"Dad? Mom? What's going on?" Neither of them speak to me. It's as if I don't exist.

I push past my mom and into Ivy's room to see it had been ransacked. Clothes are strewn wildly about, her chair upside down near the window. The pink princess lamp our grandma gave her for her seventh birthday is broken, pieces of shattered ceramic littering her desk.

What the fuck?

"What happened? Where is Ivy?" I ask, as my chest tightens.

"She's gone." Dad's tone is cold and clipped.

"What do you mean, 'gone'? Where?" I panic.

"It doesn't matter. She's gone, Chloe." Dad's voice is so full of venom; I've never heard him like this before.

I look back and forth between my parents, unable to comprehend what's going on.

"Call the police! Why are you two just sitting here?" I scream at them as if *I'm* the adult and not thirteen years old.

"If only you were pure, we could have been rid of you and kept the good one." My dad's booming voice echoes over my mother's sobs.

I stare at him, my mind swirling with questions and fear. I've known for a long time that I was an *'oops'* baby, and they never wanted me. Only Ivy ever cared. She may be only two years older, but she loves me and takes care of me better than our parents ever have.

"What did you do!?" I shriek at my parents, the accusation clear.

"What I had to do! Since you've fucked around with all of Ivy's girl friends in school, he didn't want you! He took her as payment instead, you selfish little whore!" He spews the words like venom.

Certain I had heard him incorrectly, I stumble backward, crashing into the hard plaster wall and sliding down to the floor. I pull my knees into my chest, burying my face in my hands as violent sobs wreck through my body.

*They will pay for this, and I will find her.*

Five years later

I've spent every day since Ivy was taken—sold to pay some unknown debt—training myself. Learning how to fight, how to defend myself, how to kill. All of them. Anyone involved in my sister's disappearance will die by my hands.

I taught myself how to hack into surveillance systems, even some belonging to different government agencies. Their firewalls weren't as tough as you'd think. Before I go too far in hunting down the motherfucker who took my sister, it's time for them to pay.

I pull the new luggage I purchased specifically for this day from my closet, already filled with clothes that I've never worn so that nothing appears to be missing. Tearing apart my room, I make it look like Ivy's did the night she was taken. I spill the blood I drew from my own veins only hours ago, splattering just enough to create the illusion of a struggle and an injury. When I never return to town, they'll just assume I'm dead.

Over the years, I've siphoned money from my parents' accounts as soon as I figured out how to make it untraceable. They had stacks of cash sitting in the bank from selling Ivy because, as it turns out, there never was a debt. They never even noticed when little bits here and there disappeared over time. It did, however, allow me to gather a decent nest egg. Not to mention the other rich bastards' bank accounts I was able to hack. It's cute that they think just because they're rich it means they're protected. If anything, people are more willing to sell out the rich, especially when they're assholes.

*A word of advice? Treat people with kindness.*

It's just after three in the morning when I exit my childhood bedroom. Today is the day I turn eighteen, and I've never been so excited for my birthday in my entire life. I pull the stunning stiletto pocketknives out of my waistband, the identical, weighted white marble handles with rose gold blades. They are so beautiful; I can't wait to see them covered in blood. I press the release on one knife and then the other, making sure I'm ready when I enter their room.

I silently traipse down the hall to where they lie in bed, nearly skipping in glee. When I finally reach their door, I notice it's not latched. I take a deep, steadying breath before pressing my fingertips to the wood and allowing myself to enter. Given my training and the fact that I'm so small, I rarely make any noise—which I'm incredibly thankful for right now.

I sneak over to my dad's side of the bed. Looking down at him, while I hold a blade in each hand, I wait for nerves or guilt to eat away at me. But nothing of the sort comes. Only excitement and anticipation. A twisted grin stretches across my lips as I lift the blades over my head, slashing down across his chest first. The scent of iron immediately fills the room as my father's screams echo off the walls. I clamp my hand down over his mouth just as my mother jumps up out of bed and stares at me, abject horror written across her face.

"Chloe! What are you—," her words cut off when she sees that I've sliced open her husband while she slept.

"You"—I point a blade at her—"are going to stand there like a good little puppet and watch what I do to him. Understood?" I snarl the question at her.

She shakily nods her head in agreement. I turn my attention back to the man below my knives, snot running down his face as he blubbers incoherently.

"Do you know what she's been through since you sold her?" I ask my father in song. "Let's see how much you enjoy what your daughter likely went through when you sold her to human traffickers, you fucking psycho."

I grin at the word, knowing I'm likely worse, given what I'm about to do. I raise my blades again and slash down into his groin, effectively severing his dick. He groans, biting back screams, knowing they won't help, given we're miles from the nearest neighbor. Tired of his screaming, I slice across his throat; the spray of blood a beautiful contrast of crimson against the cream wall.

"Bye bye, Daddy." I snort as I close the distance between my mother and me.

"So, Mommy dearest, what do you think you deserve for standing by and allowing him to sell my big sister? Your own daughter, you piece of shit." I snort out a pathetic laugh when she begins to stutter.

"I–, I–, I promise. I di– di– didn't have anything t– t– t– do with it!" she cries, tears streaking down her face.

"Too bad for you, I know you're full of shit. It was your idea to sell me in the first place; I've seen the conversations." I ponder my next words for a moment, tapping the bloody knife against my chin. "I just can't figure out who it was you sold her to or why they would have wanted me."

"No! Ch—" I grip her throat firmly, pressing her into the wall, cutting her off before she can give me a weak ass explanation that will only serve to piss me off further.

"Bye bye, Mommy dearest." I grin at her as I shove a blade up under her chin, through her jaw, and twist it until streams of blood pour from the gaping wound.

"Bye bye, Chloe," I say goodbye to my life and my name one last time.

Present day

The hair on the back of my neck stands up as I feel his gaze land on me from across the room—my prey, Alex Warren. The man in question is so cocky; he doesn't realize I've been tracking him for weeks, finding out just what he likes. He hasn't been drawn specifically to one physical type. He's been interested in the shy women who are out here for the first time.

I sense his approach before I feel him. His hand brushes lightly against the small of my back as if he were a gentle soul. As if, motherfucker.

"Hello, sir." I giggle shyly up at him, batting my lashes with as much innocence as I can muster.

"Hey there, babygirl." His voice is raspy like he's smoked a carton a day since he was ten. "What is a pretty little thing like you doing at a bar all on your own, especially when you could be on my arm instead?" His wink makes me internally cringe.

With my mask still firmly in place, I respond with a naive smile plastered across my lips.

"Are you offering to keep me company, sir?" I let out an innocent giggle.

"If you'll let me, babygirl." His lips twitch while his fingers trail lightly up my spine. "Let's get out of here."

BINGO.

"Sure," I respond quietly as I stand from my bar stool. He grabs my hand and gently pulls me behind him toward the lobby. "I have a room if you'd like to join me there." I lean into him, pressing my fingers softly against his chest as I gaze up through my dark lashes. With a quick nod, he veers off course from the front desk and walks toward the elevators. He always has the women get the room in their name. I just saved some time and planned ahead. Little does he know that while he was talking to escorts earlier this week, I cloned his phone while it lay on the bar. I also took it upon myself to borrow one of his credit cards while he had been distracted to book the room. I didn't want anyone to recognize that he was with me. Not that my vibrant blue hair hidden inside a dark wig and overdone makeup would really give me away.

As we enter the elevator, I press the button for the penthouse. I chose this room for a reason. I can have all the fun I crave and make it look like an accident when I'm done. The doors open to my floor, and I use my key card to access the room. After we cross the threshold, he pins me against the door as it closes behind us. I smirk up at him as his eyes darken in anticipation with each passing second. His hand creeps up between my breasts until his fingers curl around my neck.

"Take off your fucking clothes, baby girl," he snarls as he grips my throat.

A full-on grin pulls at my lips. "You first, sir," I respond coyly as I bring my knee up in a sharp, swift motion, nailing him in the crotch.

He collapses to the floor, and I kick him in the temple. His body goes slack as unconsciousness takes hold, and I get to work.

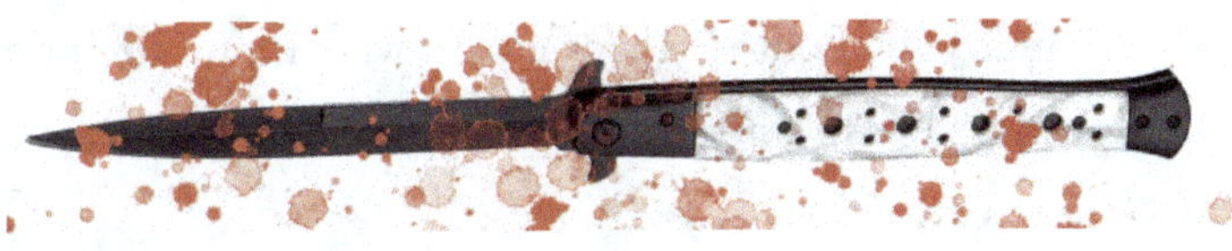

By the time he regains consciousness, it's been thirty minutes. I only noticed because he started groaning and pulling against his restraints.

"Hello, sir," I say shyly, sarcastically mimicking my demeanor from earlier. Dropping the act, I transition into a disgusted grimace. "Change of plans, motherfucker."

He growls at me through the ball gag. The sick fuck has a nice body, and if I didn't know how twisted he was with selling women, I'd probably be attracted to him. Not just what I'm going to do to him. I pull out a pre-filled syringe I had hidden in my thigh-high boots and prep it as I walk toward him. He winces as I take the protective cap off the needle and plunge it into the shaft of his limp cock. He struggles and screams into the ball gag when he feels the sharp sting of the needle and its contents. I stroke his cock a few times until the effects become noticeable.

"Ahh, there we go. Now, I can have some fun, and you can tell me what I want to know." I smile at him from between his legs and sheath his cock with a condom. I stand and remove my clothing, leaving my boots on for easier access to my weapons. Peeling my short skirt down my hips, I kick it to the side. I grin down at him as I pull my low-cut blouse up over my head before sauntering over to him and straddling his restrained body. I guide myself onto his cock and slowly pump myself up and down. The resulting groan through the ball gag has me chuckling to myself.

"Now, sir. If you will be a good boy, I'll take the ball gag out, so we can chat while I have my fun."

Mr. Warren groans and nods his head. I remove the gag, and his groans become louder. "Fuck you, you crazy bitch. I will end you." His words are cut off as I grind my hips in circles against him, a long string of curses flowing from his lips.

"Uh huh, ok. So anyway, sir," I sneer as I start to bounce a little harder. "Tell me about your operation."

"I'm not telling you shit," he hisses as I ride him faster, his breath coming quicker with my movement.

"Oh, sir. You don't have a choice. The more you deny me, the more fun I have and the less you'll have." With a wink, I pull out a blade hidden in my boots and slice across his chest. The beautiful crimson liquid glides down toward his torso. I brush my hands across the oozing wound, rubbing it across his skin, which is already starting to shine with a light sheen of sweat. I become giddy as his blood soaks into my skin.

He curses. "What the fuck is wrong with you? Did I take your sister or some shit, you fucking psycho?" He grinds his teeth as I bounce on his cock a little harder, taking myself to the brink before slowing back down.

"I like making it last," I pant out, ignoring the dig as I grind my hips against him again and shrug my shoulders. He doesn't need to know how close to the truth his question is.

His growl tells me I'm not asking the correct question.

"Oh"—I giggle—"I've been single for far too long, and rather than deal with some asshole who I'm going to have to scare off, I like to take pleasure from dickbags like you who force themselves on others, taking them without their consent." I shrug. "The blood just makes it hotter for me. Not so much for you, but as I said, this isn't about you." I slam my ass back down, taking him to the hilt.

"Why should I tell you if you're just going to torture me?" His obnoxious sneer has me chuckling to myself.

"Because if you don't give me what I want, I'll just continue doing this." I pull my blade back out from where I stashed it after the first slice and drag it across his other pec.

He screams in agony, and it's like music to my ears. I wipe my hands down his chest, the red liquid coating my fingertips. The iron scent wraps around me, making my pussy drip even more and clench around him.

"Sir. Keep telling me no, and I'm going to get at least three before I throw you off the balcony." My lips twitch as my core tightens. He struggles against me while I continue using his body for my own pleasure like he has done with so many unwilling women.

"Get the fuck off!" he snarls, straining harshly against the restraints.

"Oh, I'm going to," I moan as my first orgasm takes hold. I don't stop pumping myself up and down on his cock, riding out the climax, letting it last as long as possible. A wicked grin pulls at my lips as I finally come down, feeling his feeble attempts to jerk his legs free.

"Ahh, now you're starting to get it. You're going to tell me, or I'm going to continue injecting you with that magical little syringe until you're so hard it feels like you have dynamite exploding around your dick each time I use you as my own personal fuck toy." Picking up my knife once more, I flip it in my hand, catching the handle. The swift movements make him twitch against his restraints even more.

His eyes go wide an instant before I feel a leather-covered hand wrap around my throat.

"Don't move, Killer," the velvety smooth voice says into my ear. An intoxicating mix of whiskey and sin passes through my senses as he continues, "I just want to join in while you have your fun." He pulls a knife out of nowhere, slicing against my own chest. I scream in pleasure as I start pumping up and down on my target again.

"Who are you, Knife Daddy?" I whimper as his grip on my throat tightens, cutting off my air just enough to have me seeing stars.

"Oh, that's none of your concern yet, beautiful. The only concern you have is getting the information you need, so I can show you what a real dick can do to that pussy." He steps aside, so I can see his face, which is obscured by a black mask.

"Oh, fuck." I groan as I continue my assault on the man who is no longer my priority. The masked man towers over us. His broad shoulders and thick arms are covered by a black henley, the fabric stretching over his obvious muscles.

Without another word, he tears his belt off in one fluid motion. Unbuttoning his dark jeans, he slowly pulls out the longest and thickest cock I've ever seen, which isn't even the most impressive thing about it. I whimper when I see the metal gleam from underneath. He's pierced, and I have an overwhelming desire to feel him filling me immediately.

"Oh, fuck me, Knife Daddy," I scream as my head falls back, and I come around the target's cock again.

"Get it wet, Killer," Knife Daddy commands. I open my mouth, still riding out my pleasure, and grab the stranger's ass, pulling him into my mouth. Sucking him deep, I count six piercings in total sliding across my tongue. His responding growl as he pulls back has me near the edge again. "I said get it wet, not make me come. The first time I come in you will be after I pound your ass while you're getting what you need from this worthless piece of garbage. Once he's gone, we can discuss further orgasms for us both."

The masked man grips my throat again as he straddles my target's legs along with me, lining himself up with my ass. I slow my movements, so he can fill me. He grips my hips; the leather gloves cool against my heated skin. I feel his bare cock pressing against my tight ring before he guides himself inside.

"Oh yes, Knife Daddy!" I scream as he starts railing me while I ride my target. The balls on either side of each piercing massaging my walls make everything even more intense.

Several orgasms later and twice as many slices across my target's chest and abdomen, I have the information I need, and I slit the asshole's throat.

"That was the sexiest thing I've ever seen, Killer," my Knife Daddy says from behind me as he pulls out, backing away from me. The target's carotid sprays against my chest, and I bathe in the lifeblood of the man who took so many lives himself.

When the blood has finally stopped spurting, I stand and spin on my heel, taking my already-stained knife and pressing it to his throat.

"Who the fuck are you?"

"My friends call me AK, but I like it when you call me Knife Daddy." He chuckles and winks at me behind the mask.

"That's not what I meant, asshole, and you know it," I growl. "Who. The fuck. Are you?" Each word I spit laced with venom.

AK doesn't say anything for several moments, just stares down at me before he walks into my knife, pushing me back against the wall. His hands press flat against the rough surface on either side of me, caging me in with his large body. A small trickle of blood drips down his muscular neck, sending heat straight to my core.

"I was sent to take him out," he says flatly.

"What do you mean, 'sent'?" I raise a brow at him.

"Ahh, not yet, Killer. We can discuss that later." He grips my ass and lifts me into his arms. My legs tangle around his waist instinctively. "I believe I still have something to prove to you."

"Wha—" The words are cut off as he slides his length inside my pussy in one swift thrust. Filling me like I've never experienced before.

"Fucckkkkk, Knife Daddy," I moan so loudly my voice breaks.

"Don't worry, Killer, you won't want another dick after this." He groans in my ear while his hand still hidden beneath the leather glove snakes its way up my body and grips my throat. He squeezes tight. "You're mine now." The devilish way he pounds into me sends my nervous system into overdrive as I climax around his metal-studded length, not once or twice but three times in quick succession before I collapse against his chest as he finds his release inside me. I feel his seed dripping down my thighs as he pulls out.

"You motherfucker!" I pull back to punch him. "You didn't wear a condom!"

"I'm clean. Plus, I'd enjoy seeing you swollen with my baby."
He chuckles wickedly.

Oh, hell no.

For weeks, I have been following my target Alex Warren, a forty-seven –year-old man with a questionable past. The family who hired me brought proof that this fuck knuckle not only abducted their daughter but also killed her after she was rejected by whomever is the ringleader of their human trafficking organization. My plan has always been to kill him.

Perched up on the rooftop of the building across the street, I have a perfect view of every window from the tenth floor up to the fifteenth. He usually requests a room on the top floor. He's been heard in the past saying that the top floor is for winners; he won't be caught dead any lower.

*If only he could see himself now.*

After I received the notification that Mr. Warren booked a hotel room under his name and not the hooker he was meeting up with—which, by the way, was extremely out of character—I got to work, aiming my scope toward his room to see what I'm working with. I barely have a moment to process the goddess he entered the room with when she takes him down so effortlessly my cock instantly turns to steel.

*Fuck, she's perfection.*

When she finally finishes tying him up the way she wants, she begins to disrobe. I lose all train of thought, the job I was hired for the furthest thing from my mind. I need to see her up close and as personal as I can. She may not know it yet, but she is mine.

She takes the muted wig off, her vibrant blue locks flowing down her back, and my heart skips a beat.

Goddamn.

My mind loses the battle in staying to complete the job. Before I know it, my rifle is back in its case, and I'm taking the stairs two at a time to find out who this beautiful creature is. I reach the room to the sounds of an orgasm. My dick hasn't gone down since I first saw her, and hearing how she sounds when she comes undone has it weeping, begging me for release.

I pull a master key card from my pocket. The housekeeping woman I saw a few floors down really should keep her key cards on her person, not on her cart left in the hallway. I hold my breath as the door clicks open, hoping she won't hear. When I open the door the entire way, I'm just out of sight, and her back is facing the door. My tongue flicks out, wetting my lips in anticipation.

*So inexperienced, my little killer. This is going to be fun.*

I pull my mask down to fully cover my face before closing the distance between us. I see the man's eyes go wide as I grip her throat in my gloved hand; she freezes briefly.

"Don't move, Killer." I feel her relax at the sound of my voice. "I just want to join in while you have your fun." I grin behind my mask as I pull a blade from my jeans and lightly slice across her chest.

She screams and starts fucking the asshole again, the pain causing pleasure that I didn't expect.

*Well, fuck me, this is going to get real interesting.*

"Who are you, Knife Daddy?" She whimpers as I tighten my grip on her throat, her pleasure climbing as I cut off her oxygen.

"Oh, that's none of your concern yet, beautiful." I take a breath, making a decision that will change the course of both our lives. Releasing her throat, I round the chair to stand beside Mr. Warren. "The only concern you have is getting the information you need, so I can show you what a real dick can do to that pussy."

"Oh, fuck." She groans, her eyes taking in me in my blacked-out outfit. Black jeans, long sleeve henley, black combat boots and, of course, the mask to complete my murder ensemble.

Without another word, I unhook my belt and whip it off in one flick of the wrist, unbutton my jeans, and slowly reveal my thick length to her. Women have begged me to stop before, and usually, I do. But not with her. No, I'm going to enjoy taking her places she never knew she needed to be. Her eyes are alight with anticipation when she sees the ladder piercings glistening in the light from the underside of my dick. The soft whimper that passes her lips has me aching for her even more.

"Oh, fuck me, Knife Daddy." Her screams echo through the room, her eyes closing tight as the climax hits, her head dropping back between her shoulders as she comes down.

She's so beautiful when she comes. I know it's nothing in comparison to how she's going to look while I work her over.

"Get it wet, Killer," I instruct.

Without pause, she leans toward me, her mouth opening. She reaches out and wraps her arms around my thighs, gripping my ass. Her nails dig into my skin as she sucks me deep into her throat without hesitation. I feel my balls tighten just at the connection to her tongue. I growl, internally cursing myself for nearly finishing like some two-pump chump when there is so much more I plan to do to her.

"I said get it wet, not make me come. The first time I come in you will be after I pound your ass while you're getting what you need from this worthless piece of garbage. Once he's gone, we can discuss further orgasms for us both." I wink at her, not that she can tell with the mask.

Taking a step, I grip her throat with my gloved hand again. Angling myself, I straddle the trash she's using for her own pleasure as she extracts the information she needs from him and line myself up to her ass. She slows her movement for me. Pressing the tip of my cock against the tight ring of muscle, I ease my way inside her.

Fuck, her ass is tight as hell. I drop my hand from her throat, spreading her cheeks to give me easier access. Once I'm fully seated, she starts taking advantage of the fullness riding both of our cocks. A dark chuckle erupts from my chest as I trail my hands from her ass cheeks to her hips, gripping tightly as I thrust up into her, over and over.

"Oh yes, Knife Daddy!" She screams for me as I continue taking what I need.

I see stars when her ass tightens on my cock, strangling me as she falls over the edge again. It's a miracle I don't empty inside her immediately, but somehow, I hold off. She slices into Warren's skin every time he doesn't give her an answer she likes; rivulets of red splashed across his chest. Usually, I'm not one for blood play, but this has been hot as hell.

Another fifteen minutes of her using his body has me ready to worship the ground this gorgeous creature walks on. She's found multiple releases by the time he gives her the information she's been looking for. She slits his throat, blood trailing down his neck and chest as he fades into the welcoming darkness of death.

"That was the sexiest thing I've ever seen," I praise as I pull out of her ass, still hard as stone. I take a step back giving her some space to stand as well.

In the blink of an eye, she's standing and spins around to face me. The blade of her knife covered in Warren's blood pressed firmly against my throat.

"Who the fuck are you?" she snarls at me.

"My friends call me AK, but I like it when you call me Knife Daddy," I say, chuckling at her with a wink.

Her fury radiates through her tight little body; it's adorable.

"That's not what I meant, asshole, and you know it." Her snarl turns into a growl, "Who. The fuck. Are you?" I can tell she's trying to threaten me with her words and tone, but really, it's just making my still-stiff cock even harder.

I contemplate for a moment just how much I want to tell her as I glance down at her still-bare body. Fuck, she's perfect. Toned and tight, yet soft in all the right places. Without a word, I walk into her personal space, her blade digging into my neck. I place my hands flat on the wall behind her head, caging her in place. I feel a bead of liquid drip down my neck.

"I was sent here to take him out."

"What do you mean, *sent*?" She cocks a brow at me.

"Ahh, not yet, Killer. We can discuss that later." I lower my hands from the wall, gripping her ass and lifting her into my arms, pinning her against the wall. Her legs immediately wrap around my hips. "I believe I still have something to prove to you." I smirk as I grind my cock against her slick pussy.

Knowing I may regret this, considering I have no clue how many of her targets she's fucked or what they may have had, I can't resist the feel of her.

"Wha—" She doesn't finish the sentence before I slide home, filling her to the hilt. Fuck, her pussy feels even better than her ass.

"Fucckkkkk, Knife Daddy." Her voice cracks as the moan passes her lips.

I know I'm not going to last long with how tight her cunt is gripping me. I fuck her into the wall, thrust after thrust, punishing her pussy for ever being with another, claiming it for myself. I'll never allow her to take another man. Fuck that. She's *mine*.

I roar as I feel her convulse around me, milking every drop from my cock. I press my forehead to her neck, catching my breath for a moment before releasing her and pulling out.

When I step away from her, I can tell the moment she feels the evidence of our climaxes mixing. Her beautiful features twist into rage.

"You mother fucker!" She pulls back to punch me, but I sidestep just before it lands.

"I'm clean. Plus, I'd enjoy seeing you swollen with my baby." My grin is as wicked as my chuckle.

By the look on her face, she's contemplating how she's going to kill me.

Those icy-blue orbs glaring through my soul. She won't though. Once she calms down, she'll realize just how perfect we are for each other.

"Your eyes are gorgeous," I breathe out as I look past the anger and fear.

"Thanks, I grew them myself." She snorts out the smartass retort, pulling a laugh from deep in my chest.

Oh, yes, she's absolutely perfect for me.

It's been weeks, and I haven't been able to shake this guy. From the moment he helped me dispose of Warren's body, he's been my damn shadow. I haven't had anyone this close to me since I left home.

In his defense, after the number of times he made me come around his cock of steel that first night, I haven't really been fighting him on his vicinity. The moment he got rid of the mask, I was done for. His intense gray stare has a light of playfulness when he looks at me. His striking features caught me off guard; the man looks like he was chiseled from fucking stone, his body sculpted to perfection. I may have let him fuck me, but that was in the heat of the moment. I was already so hot; I would have fucked him even if he'd had four heads. *I was reading alien smut the other day. Don't judge me.* Sure, I give him shit and told him to leave me alone, but we both know I could get away if I really wanted to.

We've been staying at my place—well, Ivy's place. You'd think the landlord would pay more attention to who he's renting to, but I guess slumlords don't really give a shit. He's made it abundantly clear each time I've had to report issues with electrical or drywall cracking that he doesn't care.

If I'm honest, the drywall may have been me getting too rough with the woman I brought home. She said she was into orgasm denial. She changed her tune when I had her strung up against the wall and devoured her pussy like it was my last meal for hours on end, stopping just before she could climax. It was hot as hell, until she got so fed up with the denial that she tore the hook out of the wall. Although, looking back, that was pretty hot, too.

I made her come before she left. She just had to ask nicely. She'd been too demanding even before she fucked up my ceiling. A shiver runs through me at the memory.

"What is it, Killer?" AK asks from the other side of the couch, his shaggy, ash-colored hair styled in unruly waves bouncing as he turns my way.

I shake my head, ignoring the question. He doesn't need to know my secrets, at least not yet. His dark chuckle reverberates through me.

"Oh, Killer. You think you can get away with that?" He smirks. His steel gray eyes bore into my soul as he holds my gaze, his chiseled jaw flexing in the low glow of the TV. "When you're lost in thought, you chew your bottom lip. When your mind goes to filthy thoughts, your breath hitches. You were doing a bit of both, so was it me, or do I need to continue proving to you that you don't need another cock in your life, beautiful?"

I can't help the giggle that passes my lips. It's such a foreign sound that it momentarily startles me.

"No, it wasn't you, nor was it another cock." I slap his chest as he crawls the length of the couch, looming over my body.

"Why don't you share with the class then?" He leans down, nipping at my jaw, gliding his tongue to the sensitive space right below my ear, sucking lightly, making me moan.

"Fuck off, Knife Daddy," I groan in an attempt to fight off the inevitable. We both know that there is no way I won't succumb to his charm and, well, that cock is too hard to deny.

"Come on, beautiful." He nips at my ear, eliciting a moan from my lips.

"I hate you." The lie comes easily, rolling off my tongue.

"No, you don't." His chuckle is deep and dark in response.

"I was thinking about the woman I fucked who cracked the drywall," I stutter as his hands trail up my sides, leaving goosebumps in their wake.

"Hmm, and what did you do to make her crack the ceiling, Killer?" he taunts me, ghosting his fingers along my skin.

"I-I-I wouldn't let her come until she asked nicely. She was just so whiny." The words come out in breathy pants.

"Hmm," he repeats the sound. "Now, are you going to be a good girl and ask nicely, or should I see how much you can take before you tear apart the drywall?"

I whine as he continues taunting me. Writhing under his touch, the man knows how to work me like we've been together for years, not mere weeks.

"I think you can do better than that," he teases as he dips his head between my thighs nipping at the sensitive skin.

He continues his agonizingly slow torture for far too long until I succumb to his silent demands.

"Please, Knife Daddy!" I beg, "Please, fuck me, make me come."

"Good girl," he growls before he finally gives me what I need.

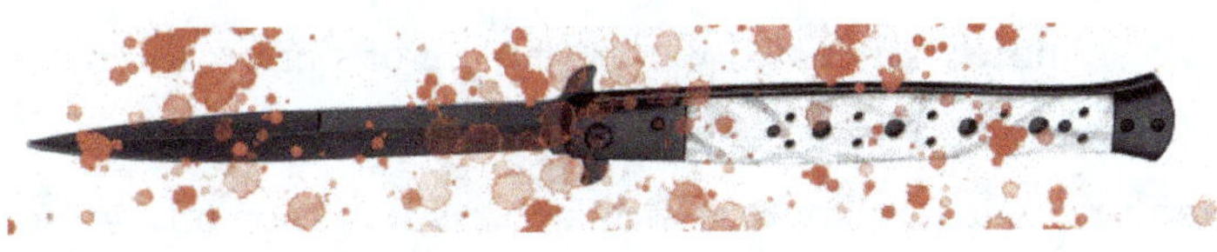

AK promised he would help me find my sister; for better or worse, he would use his connections to get her back. We've been searching for weeks and haven't found anything more than what the piece-of-shit Alex Warren provided to us during our interrogation. It's been infuriating. We've spent most of our time putting Rosalie and Emmett to shame with how active our sex life has been since we met.

We've been staring at a computer screen for the past two hours. My back leaning against his chest as we continue sifting through Alex Warren's online history and footprint. For someone who dealt in abducting and selling human beings, you would think he'd be smarter about what he did online.

His search history tells a different story. The fact that he was never under any scrutiny by the authorities only pisses me off further. When you have money and can grease the right palms, no one gives a shit about what you do. That's how my father got away with everything he did when Ivy disappeared.

"Who is that?" AK points to the screen, and I see a man who fits the description of one of the higher-ranked men than my last target, leaving the same hotel.

"I think I have something on him. Hold on." I move the mouse around the screen to open the file I created that stores every piece of information I've been able to find about anyone even remotely associated with that piece of shit organization. Clicking on an image of the man we saw on the surveillance footage, a dossier appears with a name, last known location, potential level within the organization, and any other criminal ties and aliases.

While he may not be as high up in the hierarchy as I'd like, taking him out could get me more information. It could get me closer to Ivy. I grin, tilting my head to look up at AK's beautiful face.

"How about a date night?" I giggle.

"You're not fucking another man for the rest of your life, Killer. As long as we're on the same page there, we're good to go." His returning grin has me melting back into him. He wraps his arms around my chest for a brief moment, holding me against him for a breath before releasing me. "Let's get him, beautiful."

I squeal as I leap from the couch, running into my bedroom. I quickly dress in a black, pleather skirt just long enough to hide my besties, garters that hold my blades, and a long sleeved, black crop top, putting my tits on full display. I tuck my hair under a dark wig before sauntering back to where AK stands, looking like a fucking snack no matter what he wears. It's really unfair. With one last look of appreciation over my man, I close the distance between us, placing my hand in his, and tangle our fingers together as I lead him out of my apartment.

My Killer is drenched in another man's blood. She'd been hunting on her own for years for the assholes who stole her sister, using the time to hone her craft until I came across her a few months ago on a job. Fuck, she's beautiful like this, fully immersed and in her element. The thick crimson liquid staining her porcelain skin is the perfect contrast. She refuses to keep her face hidden once we're in a confined space, so I get to see her long, blue hair cascading down her back as I watch her do what she does best.

"Killer," I scold when I see her hike up her skirt. "We've had this conversation."

"Oh, shut up. You know you're the only dick I need, Knife Daddy." She winks as she pulls out her Italian stiletto pocketknife from the garter around her thigh.

I chuckle, nodding at her to continue.

"So, Mr. Craven. I can either have more fun and take another finger, spill some more blood"—Pocket smirks up at him through her dark lashes, gliding the knife down her current target's chest—"or you can tell me what I want to know, we can end this now, and I can fuck my man while you bleed out." Her voice is seductive, but her wide grin speaks volumes to me. She wants him to fight it. She lives for the pain she inflicts on these pieces of shit. By the time I get my hands on her, she won't just be drenched in the man's blood. I will find a puddle between her thighs. The thought has my cock stiffening in my pants. I groan, ready to take over.

"Killer," I call out to Pocket, my voice full of lead. She turns around with a pout on her face.

"But I was just starting to have fun!"

"I'll make sure you have fun after we get what we came here for, beautiful." I walk behind Mr. Craven, facing her and pulling my mask up just enough to show her my mouth. My lips twitch into the lopsided grin I know makes her putty in my hands. I hear her soft moan as she steps back, submitting to my desire. I pull the mask back down, chuckling, and return to standing in front of the man of the hour.

"Let's get down to it, shall we?" I inject venom into the words to get my point across. "Give me the names of anyone associated with the organization that sells the women," I snarl.

"I don't know what you're talking about," Mr. Craven sputters, his eyes wild, looking around the room for anything that might save him. Newsflash: there's nothing.

"Do you want me to call the lady over here? While I enjoy getting my hands dirty, she gets off on it more than I do. I'll have my fun with her long after you're gone." I pat his face with my leather-covered hand as I step away, allowing Pocket access. She raises both of her blades into view before she slashes them down in an X motion across his bare chest.

"Oh, god!" he cries out. "It's Hymen, Johnny Hymen!"

With a wide grin brightening her face, I see the moment my Killer's need to draw blood is satiated.

"You're up, Knife Daddy." She walks back to me, running her nails down my chest. "I wanna see you work."

I snicker as I grip her hair, wrapping it tightly around my fist as I peer down at her.

"As you wish, Killer."

I drag her along, the soft moans going straight to my dick. *Fuck me.* I force her to her knees in front of me and Mr. Craven.

"Eyes on me," I command as I retrieve my toys. Usually, I like to be direct and to the point once I have the information I came for. My girl, though, she needs more. When my blade passes through the dorsalis pedis artery, the smallest, just enough pressure to nick it, blood starts to pool around his feet where I made the cuts. While my killer may have a blood kink, I prefer a quick shot through the skull. It makes for a quicker exit and less cleanup. However, the whimper that escapes her perfectly pouty lips every time she catches sight of the crimson liquid sends a jolt straight to my dick. I move from his feet up to the femoral artery on his other leg, and my knife slices through his skin like butter.

"Yes, Knife Daddy," Pocket moans next to me. She raises her hands to my thighs, squeezing me tightly. I look down at her while Mr. Craven slowly bleeds out, the universe taking pity on his sorry ass as he sits unconscious in the chair.

I tear off my mask as she unbuckles my belt, undoing my pants and freeing my cock in record time.

"Take me in your mouth, Killer." I smirk at her as I jam my blade through his carotid. The blood barely spews, just enough to satisfy her kink.

Without saying a word, she tongues each piercing before wrapping her lips around my thick rod. She takes me to the back of her throat in one swift motion. There's no point in stifling my groan. We're far enough away from people in this house that we have privacy.

"Jesus Christ." I pant as she grips my ass, holding on as she fucks me with her mouth. Her nails dig in when I fist her hair, tightening my grip to hold her still, so I can take back some control, thrusting in and out of her hot, wet mouth until my balls tighten. I force her off me. "Up, now," I demand and wink at her.

"Yes, Daddy," she purrs as she climbs to her feet. I lift her into my arms, my hands cupping her ass, massaging her cheeks as I carry her to the couch across from Mr. Craven's remains. I toss her down and drop to my knees, ready to worship my Killer. I push the tiny excuse of a skirt she's wearing up over her hips, exposing her bare ass. I growl.

"Woman, how many times have I told you not to go out like this?" I snarl at her, pulling out a knife from my black jeans.

"It just makes it easier for you"—she giggles at me—"make it hurt."

I growl as I bury my face in her pussy, lapping up her soaking wet cunt. I open our knife. The knife we've reserved for use solely on each other. It's a breathtaking piece. The blade is black titanium. A dandelion blowing a wish into the wind is engraved on the custom finishing which folds into a stunning coralwood handle when we're not using it. I slice it across the top of her right thigh. As her blood drips down her leg, I feel her grip my hair, pulling me closer. I move my tongue faster, paying close attention to her clit. I swirl circles around her swollen nub, flicking and sucking it hard in my mouth as her body tenses. I hold the blade of our knife in my leather-clad hands, bringing it between her legs and sliding the cold handle inside her perfect little pussy.

"Oh fuck, Daddy. Don't stop." Her screams only drive me wild; tormenting myself with her pleasure can be a real bitch. Slowly sliding the handle in and out a few times, bringing her right to the edge as I pull her clit between my teeth, nibbling gently, her thighs clenching around my head like a vice for more. I chuckle against her sopping mound, peeling her legs off me one at a time.

I stand to align my aching cock to her tight entrance, grinning at her as I slowly guide myself inside, filling her one piercing at a time until I'm fully seated inside of her. Before I move, I bring the blade to my face, running my tongue along the handle, tasting the juices still present. Her walls tighten around me as I flip the knife in my hand and catch the handle in one fluid motion, bringing it down to her other thigh, making a longer cut before I start pounding her. She screams, the pain and pleasure mixing with each thrust.

"Fuck me, Knife Daddy. Fuck me," she begs as I continue my assault. "Don't fucking stop."

I snake one arm up her body, gripping her throat. Her eyes roll back into her skull while my other hand finds her swollen nub, pinching it between my fingers and sending her over the edge. Her climax tears through her, her already tight pussy strangling my cock as her crescendo continues for several moments before I find my own release, filling her with yet another load.

AK and I have been at this for weeks since we finally found a lead with Mr. Craven. AK had taken the job that brought us together a couple of months ago now, and after our meet cute when he had been tracking Alex Warren, we haven't been apart for more than a few hours. We've been waiting, working toward ending the human trafficking organization that destroyed my life. We climb closer to the top of the food chain with each asshole we take out. Our date night with Mr. Craven last week ended with some decent information and multiple amazing orgasms. My man has me dickmatized.

I would find the irony funny that the motherfucker's name is Hymen when he only takes virgins, but I've seen the aftermath of the bodies when they're found. I can't wait to dig my blades into his flesh, letting him feel the steely weight as the metal doles out my bloody vengeance. I'm giddy at the thought of peeling his skin from his body so that his insides are on the outside. I may not take full advantage of my targets anymore, but my man will have to deal with me at least touching his dick a few times.

I've been searching for my big sister for years. The day I turned eighteen, I left home to find her because the cops didn't care, and our parents are the ones who sold her. They told the authorities she ran away and had her declared dead after a year of being gone. Like fuck she ran away. By the time I got a lead, it all pointed to this organization.

I had scoured the darkest depths of the internet for disappearances similar to Ivy's when I came across this piece of shit Hymen Corp. They specialize in procuring virgins to sell off to the highest fucking bidders. I swore that I'd do everything I possibly could to find her, to save as many of them as I could.

"Beautiful?" AK's voice pulls me from the thoughts of my past.

I look in the mirror I've been standing in front of and see him standing across the room, admiring my black bodycon midi from behind. His ashy hair is slicked back; he looks gorgeous, as always, but so out of the norm for what I've become accustomed to.

"I'm here, Knife Daddy"—I sigh—"just lost in the past for a second. Let's go."

He closes the distance between us and grabs my hand, spinning me around and pulling me into his chest. I look up into his breathtaking steel gray eyes. His face is so perfectly sculpted; he could be one of Michelangelo's masterpieces.

"I promised I would help you find out what happened to her. We're getting closer." He brushes a rogue strand of hair off of my face. "I will do everything I can to help you paint the world red with their blood until every last one of them is gone."

His beautiful lips form the lopsided grin that does things to me I can't control.

"Ugh, Knife Daddy." I moan into his neck. "Unless you're gonna make it hurt, you can't do that to me!"

"Later, Killer. I just like to keep you on your toes." I groan, pulling away and craning my neck to look into his eyes again. I press my lips to his, looping my arms around his neck. His hands wrap around me, one hand cupping my ass, the other fisted in my hair, giving a firm tug, making me melt against him with the tease of pain. My mouth parts for him, allowing him access. The way he works me over with the sensual flicks and swirls as our tongues collide has me wishing I had put panties on. I'm already dripping down my thigh for him. I groan into his mouth as he squeezes my ass harder before he pulls away and lowers me to the ground.

"Come on." He winks as he pulls away.

Motherfucker knows exactly what he's doing. I follow along like the good girl I am for him. Only for him.

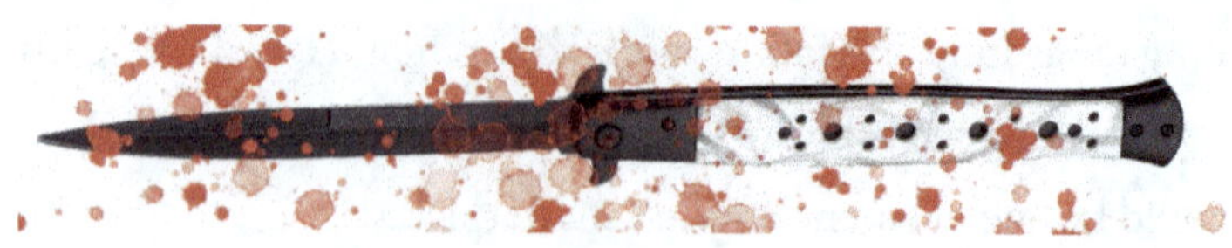

"So this dress. You bought it for me to wear to dinner?" The concept foreign to me.

"Yes, Killer. Why else do you think I would have picked something so restricting?"

"I don't know, I thought you were trying to test my skill set," I admit.

AK chuckles at me as I glance around the restaurant. I'm not sure how to act. I've never gone out to dinner with a man before. I've had multiple meals with this man since we've met, and he has refused to leave my side, but this feels different somehow.

"Why are we here?" I cock a brow at him.

"I wanted to take you on a date," he says and flashes his lopsided grin that makes me weak as I take a sip of the wine we ordered. "Our beginning was unique, but I still wanted the chance to wine and dine you. If I'm honest, I also want to show off the smokeshow I have on my arm."

I choke on the liquid at his declaration. "You and I both thrive in the shadows. Why the hell would you want to make a scene so that people notice either of us?"

"Beautiful, I will kill everyone in this room without a second thought if I think they pose a threat. I just want to show off what's mine." He grins at me.

I roll my eyes at him, not bothering to hide the smirk that pulls at my lips.

He orders for both of us, taking this entire *'you're mine'* thing to the extreme. What's shocking is I don't exactly hate it.

I start to relax as the wine settles into my system. My senses aren't muted enough, though, to miss the whispered altercation on the other side of the restaurant. A byproduct of my childhood trauma, my heightened senses allow me to notice things others overlook. I scan the restaurant in an attempt to locate the source of the quiet argument.

I sense her before I see her. They walk past our table, and while I don't catch a glimpse of his face, I do see hers and, my god, is she stunning. The woman is gorgeous; she looks to be about my age, a little shorter than me, thin but her curves are soft. Her light brown hair is styled in subdued waves, and the icy blue dress she's wearing looks like it's barely hanging on her slender frame.

My attention is solely focused on the couple as they exit the restaurant, my senses tingling, telling me something is wrong. My feet take control of my body, following behind them, not realizing I've left my date at the table. It's not until I hear his voice calling behind me that I remember his existence, losing the couple as they round a corner. My heart stutters in my chest as she vanishes from sight.

The wine we ordered is slowing my reaction time immensely. I don't realize that Pocket is gone until she's at the door. How the hell she's so goddamn fast when she's had as much to drink, if not more, than I have is beyond me. I shove my hand into my pocket, gripping everything I brought with me, and throw a wad of cash down on the table as I stand to race out after her.

Without hesitation, I make a left out of the restaurant. It's like she's a beacon calling to my soul. I know exactly where to go to find her. Running down the sidewalk as fast as my feet can carry me, I round the corner to see her blue hair flying behind her as she runs further from me. She finally comes to a halt a few yards away.

"Killer, what's going on?" I call after her as I close the distance, realizing that we've just run a few blocks from the restaurant.

Pocket is looking around frantically, her eyes darting around the buildings, windows, alleyways, cars, anywhere that she notices a flicker of movement.

I step in front of her, cutting off her line of sight to her surroundings. She finally looks up at me just long enough to register that I'm speaking to her for a brief moment.

"She's in trouble. I know she is." She looks so panicked, the words tumbling from her mouth in rapid succession. "I could see it in her face, in her response to how he spoke to her."

We haven't known each other long, but something in whatever she saw back there has scared the shit out of her.

"Ok, tell me what you saw." I attempt to remain calm. I've never been a shoulder to cry on for anyone; I've just fucked and moved on. She's different though. I can't imagine not being a support system for her. "We can't find her without breathing through this and talking it out, beautiful." I press my palm to her cheek, slowly running my hand down the side of her face before lifting her chin with my fingers.

She shudders under my touch.

"I'm right here with you." I attempt to keep my tone calm to reassure her.

"The girl was beautiful. Her hair was so long, you'd have fun holding onto it, if she let you. Her dress was too big on her, but it was the perfect shade of ice blue hanging on her tiny frame." She's staring through me as if she can still see the woman she's talking about.

"She was maybe a little older than me, I couldn't tell by how much. She was walking like she had on stilettos, so she's a little shorter than me, maybe five foot even." Pocket's icy blue eyes are locked on me as tears begin to fall down her flawless face. "He was threatening her. I couldn't make out the specific words, but her body language was screaming for help."

"Ok, which way did they go?" I look around for any sign of life, seeing none. I glance back at her.

"I think they drove off," she groans. "They were gone by the time I got to this corner, but I heard an engine revving, headed in the opposite direction."

Pocket is pacing back and forth in front of me as I dig my burner out of my slacks and send a quick text to a friend who can run a search on missing persons.

"AK, we need to find her." Pocket's voice returning to the confident, determined tone I've become accustomed to.

"Ok, let's go." I wrap my arm around her waist and drag her alongside me to where we parked.

"Where the hell are we going?" she snaps at me.

"Back to your place. I have someone checking missing persons for her description, and we will see what we can find from your surveillance software." I attempt to soothe her by detailing a concrete plan, knowing the structure will alleviate some of her agitation.

"Fine, but I want the name of whoever the fuck you're trusting with this," she snarls. "In case you forgot, we haven't known each other long enough to be sharing contacts."

"Killer, I know you're worried, but I told you when we met, you're mine now. I will take care of this, and we will get to her." I keep my tone as calm as I can even though I want to throw her against the wall and show her just how much she shares with me without even realizing it.

Once we're back to my car, I open the passenger door for her, allowing her to sit and snap her seatbelt in place before rounding the hood and taking my place behind the wheel. It's a fairly short drive back to her apartment, for which I'm thankful. Her desire to help this unknown person is doing things to my cock I didn't expect. Since when does concern do it for me?

I don't even get the car in park before she's out and racing up the stairs to her front door. I follow closely after her, unsure what I'm going to do.

I race into my apartment, the door still wide open, waiting for AK to traipse in behind me like the cute killer puppy he is. Who the hell am I kidding? I'm falling for the sexy-as-fuck pain in my ass. As soon as I reach my couch, I plop down, grabbing the laptop from the coffee table in front of me and setting it on my legs.

The screen comes to life the instant I tap the mouse pad, and I open the access point I've secured of local security cameras. When I find the cameras surrounding the restaurant, I play back several hours before we had arrived at the restaurant. AK appears in the doorway, his face an odd mixture of amusement and concern.

"You're always sexy, but something about how determined you are to get to this woman is doing things to me." He chuckles.

"You're not getting in my pants right now, Knife Daddy." I roll my eyes at him, irritated that he only seems to be thinking with his dick.

He sits next to me, trying to get close while I concentrate on the camera feeds. I try my best to actively ignore him, my eyes glued to the screen as I continue cycling through until I see her face. We've been home twenty minutes. Almost an hour since she disappeared. The fear on her face is even more obvious on the video.

"There!" I point to the screen.

My heart is hammering in my chest as I stare at her retreating form. She's just trying to survive, doing what she's told.

"She looks fucking terrified." AK's voice is venomous now that he's seen her.

"You thought I was just being dramatic?" I snarl at him. "I don't give a shit about most people after what my parents did, but she's in trouble, motherfucker. So glad you believe me now."

"Whoa, Killer. You're not dramatic. I just didn't get a good look at her to see what you did." He tries to soothe my attitude with his charm.

Of course, it works. That lopsided grin could have me admitting to all the shit I've done and turning myself over to the police if he asked, and that fact scares the shit out of me. I take a deep breath, centering myself before I respond.

"Fine." I groan. "If you want to be helpful now that you've seen it, what has your person found out, Superman?"

I type furiously on the keyboard of my laptop in an attempt to do facial recognition on the girl. The search's progress bar seems to take forever to load before popping up with zero results. Fuck. I expand the search criteria, that damn bar taking its sweet time again, when AK speaks.

"There aren't any recent missing persons reported fitting her description. At least none they could find." He huffs out a breath.

I roll my eyes at the information or rather lack thereof. Of course they haven't found anything. They aren't looking deep enough. They never think big enough. It's at that moment that my computer dings, and the screen lights up, flashing with an image of a fifteen-year-old girl and a mockup of what she'd look like today. The original image looks so familiar, but I can't quite place her.

She was reported missing a week after Ivy, only a few miles from our house. I look at the name and do a double take as memories begin flooding my mind. *Holy shit.* Echo Larson. I had a crush on her when I was younger. She used to go to school with Ivy; they were inseparable from the moment they met in pre-k. Everyone who met Echo loved her. Though, now that I think back, her parents weren't the ones who reported her as missing. It was her grandmother who insisted something had happened to her. The police humored the old woman for a week or two, but then Echo's name disappeared from everything. I haven't thought about her in years.

"Those motherfuckers!" I scream as I push my laptop away.

AK immediately catches it before it tumbles to the floor.

"Beautiful, what did you find?" He places the computer out of reach on the coffee table, probably in the hope that I won't smash it in my fury.

"I remember." I glance up at him through wet lashes, realizing only now that tears have been pooling in my eyes. "I remember her. She disappeared only a week after Ivy did. They buried her case or closed it. I don't know, I had forgotten about her. It's been so long."

I look at the computer sitting there, taunting me.

"Her parents didn't do anything, just like mine. It was her grandmother who reported her missing," I explain, "I remember now thinking back, I had been so upset about Ivy, it didn't register that it was weird."

"You're thinking her parents sold her, too?" He cocks a brow at me.

I don't respond. Not sure what I can say.

"Killer"—I feel his hands on my thighs as he kneels in front of me—"you're shaking."

I blink away the tears, refocusing my gaze, only to find worried lines marring his beautiful face. Without another word, he raises his hands to my jaw, cupping it gently. I close my eyes, so unfamiliar with the closeness he's offered since we've met. Leaning in, he presses his forehead to mine—a sweet gesture I've not experienced with him in our limited time together—before pulling away slowly. His steel grey eyes meet mine.

"Let me pull you from the darkness, beautiful." I can hear the smile in his voice.

I barely nod in response before his lips are crashing against mine. He presses his body so close to me, caging me against the back of the couch. I melt into him, parting my lips with a gasp when I feel his warm tongue swipe on my skin.

"You're not alone anymore, Killer," he whispers against my lips. "I may not have been here from the beginning, but I will be here through the end. I won't let you go."

The van's cold metal sends chills through my body, my arm pressed against the sliding door. I pull my knees to my chest as I wait for instructions. I didn't mean to upset him. I don't know why he took me with him. It's not that it was the first time he's taken me out, but it was the first time since they killed her.

They broke us both a long time ago, but with how much they used us over the years, I never thought they'd kill either of us. As long as we put up a little bit of a fight, they get off and get out.

Tears stream down my face as I remember my friend. She was full of love, even with everything we'd been through. Right up until the end, she was the most loving person and would have done anything for me. Anything that they'd allow, at least. Granted, that wasn't much, but her kindness helped get me through some of my darkest days since being taken.

"What is your problem? You wouldn't have been dragged out like that had you not been such a fucking idiot," Chris snaps at me.

His thick hair is slicked back out of his face with too much product. He looks like a child playing dress up in his dad's clothes.

"I'm sorry, sir. I didn't mean—" A sting across my face cuts off my words. The loud thwack right before impact doesn't even make me flinch anymore. I'm used to the action.

"Save your bullshit apologies for someone who believes you," he barks at me as the van comes to a sudden stop, and Chris disappears out of his side.

Once the back doors are open, I can see we've returned to the place I've called my home. Or my hell, same thing really. For the last twelve years, this place has been my sanctuary, my hell, my everything. Seeing it from this angle is always a much different experience than when I'm shoved back inside.

Chris must realize what thoughts are running through my mind because his face turns into a cocky grin.

"Time to lose the glass slipper, Cinderellie." He grips my bicep, digging his fingers into my flesh as he pulls me from the back of the van, exposing me to the elements.

The crisp evening air sends a chill through me as soon as I steady myself on my feet.

He shoves me toward the front door, his roughness throwing me off balance. I stumble over my own feet just barely catching myself and standing upright as I take the walk of shame back up to the luxurious house. If only I knew its luxury. The first time I walked through these halls was only five years ago. It took a while, but eventually, they finally trusted us enough to let us out of the room we've been imprisoned in since waking up here.

Those first seven years were spent crushing the people we once were. I guess they figured if we hadn't tried to run by then, they could trust us enough to allow us a taste of freedom. Physically, we had changed so much since we were taken; they felt it was safe enough that no one would recognize us. When we stepped into the main house for the first time, Ivy and I startled in amazement at how beautiful the inside was. It looks like royalty could live here with how elegant and fancy everything is. But it was all for show. The deepest levels of this house were where nightmares lived in the flesh.

Chris shoves me back in the room where they keep me if they're pleased with my performance, I get to roam the space freely. If they're unhappy with me, then I get confined to a hook that's anchored into the brick walls. I look across the room, the hook the only thing holding my attention. A shudder involuntarily runs through my body; the hook terrifies me every time they force us onto it. They hurt us over and over again, passing us back and forth between them. Or well, they *did* before they killed her. Now it's just me, at least until they find someone to replace her. I dig my heels in, locking myself in place when I feel him looming over me.

"You want to make this hard, Little Duck? You can either go willingly or I will remind you who is really in charge," he growls into my hair as he presses his disgusting length into my ass.

I tense, already knowing that I will not win. Standing under the hook, my hands held in front of me, I prepare myself to be strung up.

"One of these days, I'm going to shove your pussy onto that hook and see if you can survive. Your girl sure as hell didn't, she barely lasted five minutes before it ripped her apart." He snorts.

Instead of speaking, I hold my hands out, allowing him to place the binds around my wrists. He lifts the left, cuffing it in the restraint before yanking the chain on the other side, jerking my arm above my head. He finishes his task with my right wrist before smirking at me.

"Don't worry, Little Duck." His wink makes my stomach's contents want to revolt, "I'll be back to take what I want later."

*Somehow, one day. I will kill all of them.*

Chris exits the room, leaving me on my own again. I feel the tears streaking down my face. Anger rolls through my body, and I feel my blood boil. I will not die like she did. I will not roll over and allow them to finish me off, throw me out like garbage. I will fucking end them first.

From my spot in the shadows, I watch as the tall, well-dressed man walks through the alley. His terrible attempt at covert ops has me nearly snorting in disbelief.

*Is he serious?*

Rolling my eyes before making my move, I sneak up behind the guy, who I know to be Chris from my digital sleuthing. Doing my best Johnny Lawrence impersonation, I sweep the guy's leg out from under him in one swift movement. The wind is knocked out of him when he lands on his back in front of me, and I jump up, wrapping my thighs around his neck, incapacitating him easily with a triangle choke. I check to make sure he's still breathing, even though he's unconscious. My fully-custom, modified van appears with my man in the driver seat.

I grin at him with my prize at my feet before he climbs through the back to help me lift the man into the cargo space. AK collars and chains the piece of shit to the floor before putting the false back up on both sides, leaving Chris fully engulfed in darkness.

"What a fucking idiot. This fucker has left his location on everywhere he's been since we last saw him," I announce as I scroll through his phone's history. My blood pressure rises as I read through his previous searches. "A real fucking gem." I recite an address for AK to put in our encrypted GPS as the streetlights pass by, and we enter the interstate.

"What do you say we have some fun when we find her?" He smirks.

"Are you crazy? I may want your cock more than my next breath, but there's no way she'd be down for that." I lock my eyes on his.

"Killer, that's not what I was referring to." He chuckles at my protective nature over Echo. "Besides, the kind of fun I have in mind will be just as satisfying. For you, at least. I'm not sure about her yet."

He knows I'll cave. I always cave for him.

I raise a brow and shrug. Knife Daddy always knows just how to convince me.

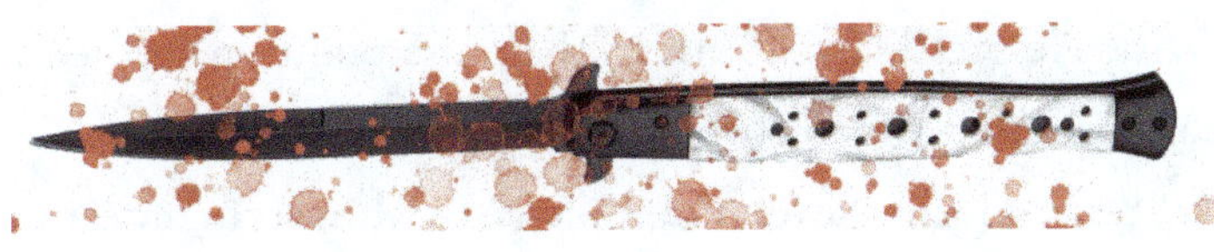

I wake up in the passenger seat of the cargo van to a muffled scream. I glance over at AK, who is tapping his fingers against the steering wheel to the beat of Tattered and Torn by Slipknot. I smile when I see he's got his ear buds in to keep from disturbing my rest. I sit up, looking at the passing surroundings, and place a hand on his thigh, his own covering mine almost immediately.

"How close are we?" I ask, rolling my neck to stretch out the kinks of sleeping in the car.

"Just a few more minutes." He smirks at me when he sees I'm raising a brow.

We pull up to a fucking castle several minutes later, my breath catching in my lungs at the sight before me.

"You can't be serious?" I scoff.

"Well, now seeing him bleed may be more pleasurable, knowing this is what they get from the people they've sold." A deep growl reverberates through his chest, echoing around the interior of the vehicle.

The van comes to a stop, and I step out to look around. We're in a secluded area, miles of rolling hills are all you can see in the distance.

Hmm, I could get used to a view like this.

AK comes up behind me, wrapping his arms around my waist. He presses a soft kiss to the pulse point on my neck, causing shivers to run down my spine.

"You ready for the real fun, Killer?" he whispers in my ear.

"Yes, Knife Daddy," I chirp in response, and I clap my hands in excitement.

AK is already back in the van, removing the false back to reveal the man from earlier. I smile at him when I step into the cargo space.

"Are you ready for some fun?" I giggle as I approach him.

It takes longer to get the man out of the van than it took to get him in it now that he's awake and clearly unhappy with his current predicament. Every time AK turns his back to grab something, he begs me to help him. After about five minutes of struggling, I pull my knife out of my boot.

"You may think he's the one you need to worry about because he's the big bad man," I croon, dragging the tip of my blade down his cheek. "But sweetheart. I'm the one who likes to bathe in blood." I wink at him before kicking him in the temple, disorienting him enough for AK to pick him up without a fight and carry the dumbass over his shoulder.

As we step through the entry of the luxurious home, I gasp at the grandeur of the foyer. An intimidating staircase that even Scarlett O'Hara would envy greets us. I stand frozen in place as I glance around the impressive space. AK startles me as he walks up behind me, slapping my ass.

"His phone's GPS says he was underground quite a bit the night and days following his last appearance," I quietly announce as I retrace his steps.

Pocket is walking at my side as I carry the limp bag of bones over my shoulder down the hall. Our steps echo along the white marble floors as she leads us down a wide corridor, coming to a bottleneck when we reach a door.

"It looks like it's this way." She shrugs as she tries the handle.

Nothing happens, and upon further inspection, we realize it requires a fingerprint. I chuckle, turning around with my back to the door so she can lift Chris' hand to cover the sensor. With an audible click, the door opens.

We slowly descend the stairs, and when we reach the bottom, Pocket turns her gaze back at me.

"It wants another fingerprint," she whispers.

I turn back around, allowing her to put his finger on this sensor as well. This time, the door creaks open like some horror movie jump scare is about to happen.

When we finally get inside and close the door, I hear Pocket let out a gasp. I follow her gaze to the other side of the room where a tiny figure is hanging from a fucking hook, like a piece of meat at a slaughterhouse.

She races to the tiny figure who screams like a banshee the moment Pocket's hand grazes her skin as she attempts to check for a pulse.

"Echo, It's ok. They won't hurt you anymore." I've never heard Pocket sound so nurturing or compassionate. My dick instantly stands tall, enjoying the sight of my woman trying to free this stranger.

*What the fuck, this isn't the time.* I admonish my cock, but he doesn't listen.

The girl is still screaming when Pocket kneels in front of her, placing her own face right in front of the girl's.

"I promise you; I will not let them hurt you. We're going to get you out of here." Pocket's voice is so soothing. "Where are the keys?"

"He always has them on him," Echo croaks like she hasn't spoken in days.

Pocket watches me as I saunter toward the metal chair that appears to be bolted to the center of the floor, slightly reclined with a curved seat. I plop him onto the metal with a clang. Pocket closes the distance between us to help me tie his arms behind him. I zip tie his ankles to the legs of the chair as Pocket pats him down, finding a single key hanging off a silver chain around his neck.

She snaps it, yanking it from his unconscious body before returning to Echo who is whimpering in anticipation of freedom.

I keep my eyes on Chris as she releases the girl. Echo collapses into Pocket's waiting arms, my woman supporting her completely. Pocket cuddles her close, gently stroking her back while whispering into her hair.

"It's ok, Sunshine. We'll make sure after tonight that he's no longer a problem," I call over my shoulder to her.

Once Echo is resting on the couch across from where Chris is strapped down, my girl makes herself comfortable. Pocket sheds her hair tie, her long, bright blue hair cascading down her back, reaching just above her ass. I can't help but smirk at her as she gets into her element. She shrugs off her jacket, laying it across the armchair by the door. I'm shocked at how much of a homey vibe this dungeon has to it. Because let's face it, that's exactly what this is—a fucking torture chamber for the rich and depraved.

I can tell the moment she sees it, really takes it in. Her eyes widen, and her lips turn up into the most beautiful grin.

"Can we play with that?" She bounces on her toes in excitement.

"We will, after he talks." I bite back a chuckle as I see Echo shifting uncomfortably in her seat.

"Yes, please!" Her excitement is contagious as she walks over to study the hook Echo was hanging from. The sharp piece of iron only serves to highlight the fucked-up shit that happens here, and my stomach turns slightly as I stare at it. The thing looks like something Captain Hook might've had if he were into some kinky shit.

Pocket walks over to Chris and slaps him across the face, bringing him fully back into consciousness.

"What the fuck!?" the man screams when he comes to. "Where the fuck am I? Who the fuck are you?"

"Awe, you're cute when you're confused." Pocket giggles, then continues, "I'm Pocket, and this is AK. Not that that really matters. You won't be around long enough to use our names," she explains, her voice coming out in a singsong.

"So, Chris"—I clear my throat—"we know you work with a human trafficker. What we need to know is how to find him."

"Fuck you. I'm not telling you shit, psycho!" He spits at Pocket, the sputum landing on her favorite leather boots.

"Oh, buddy. That was the wrong move." My grin turns positively evil, and venomous rage rips through my veins.

Pocket wipes the spit on Chris's pants. With no words passing between us, in one swift movement, she brandishes her favorite blade and presses it to his jugular. Echo's maniacal giggle pulls my gaze away from my Killer. I look back at her, and she's sitting on the edge of her seat visibly vibrating with excitement.

An expression somewhere between torment and elation has taken over her gorgeous features.

"And here I thought you would be a good boy and not test us." The wicked smile on Pocket's face has my cock threatening to burst through my pants.

He swallows hard against the blade, and a tear falls from his eye.

"I don't know where he is," he cries out, pathetic desperation coating the words.

"I think you're lying. From the text messages we found on your phone, it looks like you saw him recently." Pocket continues her fun, slicing tiny cuts across his chest. She's so fucking good with a knife that she can inflict something resembling a paper cut with a blade.

"I swear! I may have seen him, but it wasn't where he stays!" Chris's voice cracks with a sob when the blade opens his skin again.

"Try again." I smirk, my eyes drifting to the hook.

"Oh, fuck. You're both insane!" he screams. "HELP! SOMEONE HELP!"

Pocket's eyes find mine from where she stands, and we both start laughing like we're watching George Carlin live. She's bent over, unable to catch her breath from laughing so hard. I'm not any better, barely holding myself up, and laughter breaks free from my chest. Chris is staring at us, terror filling his expression.

I'm not sure how long it takes to catch our breath before we can get back to why we brought him here.

"Killer, do you want blood or no blood tonight?" I ask Pocket, who is still clearly amused at Chris' plea for help. Chris' eyes dart back and forth between us in confusion.

"Blood," she states, her smile wide. "Always blood."

Several hours of interrogation later, we feel like Chris has given us all we're going to get. His skin is so pretty with cuts from my knife marring his chest and torso. Now, for the part I've been eagerly awaiting. I look over to Echo who is sitting on the couch, literally on the edge of her seat, watching us with curiosity and excitement lighting her eyes.

"How about we allow some penetration before we say good-bye, yea?" My giggle is wicked as I turn to Echo. "Do you want to have a slice or two before we make it real painful?"

She nods enthusiastically but stares at AK's menacing form, not moving.

"It's ok, Little Spark." I smile at her, the same smile I gave her all those years ago when I was still just a kid she'd never look twice at. "He won't hurt you. If he tries, I'll do worse than what we're about to do to this trash bag."

She looks at me, a question in her captivating jade eyes that she doesn't voice, before she takes a steadying breath and nods, walking toward me. She wraps herself around me as I guide her over to where Chris is restrained. She's absolutely terrified of AK, which both worries me and pisses me off. I'm angry for the person she once was, someone who would have given the shirt off her own back, to be reduced to this meek, timid woman, too terrified to even speak.

When we reach the chair, I hand her my stiletto pocketknife. The cool blade laying against my skin, I offer a smirk and a wink before she takes the handle. She untangles herself from me just long enough to carve a long slice from his pec to just above his groin. She slashes him so deeply he starts convulsing, and I shudder at the image. She's going to be a lot of fun once she's got a handle on her emotions.

"Fuck you, you piece of shit. For everything you've done to us. For taking us the way you did and for killing her in such a brutal way, you psychopath!" Echo screams the first words she's spoken since we arrived. She's shaking, her emotions finally breaking free.

"Who did he kill, Sunshine?" AK asks before I get the chance. He makes sure to stay as far away from us as he can.

"My best friend. We'd been here for so long," she stutters, her breath catching as she tries to find the words. "They hung her," she cries as her eyes collide with the hook I've been looking forward to using.

"Stand behind me, Echo. We're going to return the favor." I smirk at her as I take her hand, tucking her behind my back, so AK and I can get Chris into position.

We carefully unhook the restraints one by one, being sure to dislocate each of his limbs, so he can't run before the next one is released. The pop and cracking sounds of each joint are like music to my ears, my smile widening with each snap. He's sobbing in pain by the time we raise him to the hook I've been staring at so lovingly throughout the interaction. I can't wait to see how long he lasts.

AK is holding the majority of the weight as I climb up and slap Chris' cheeks before spreading them wide to make sure we get it in the right hole. Though it looks sharp enough that it wouldn't necessarily matter. Once I have them lined up, AK slowly pushes Chris backward onto the hook. His earsplitting screams as the metal tears through him sends shivers down my spine. We use ropes to suspend his upper body from the ceiling since we don't want him to be torn apart too quickly. That would ruin the fun for the rest of our date night.

I press a soft kiss against AK's lips, before returning to Echo's side. I pull her into my chest, holding her as we enjoy the show. Chris continues screaming as he struggles against the hook and ropes, blood trickling down his chest from the stunning work of my blade and streams of the beautiful crimson liquid flowing from his ass the more he fights.

I squeal with glee with every scream Chris lets out.

"Killer, remind me not to piss you off." AK shivers next to me, still maintaining some distance while I hold Echo close.

"Unless you cheat on me or go down the path these fuckers have"—I turn to face him, smiling as I take in his beautiful face—"you don't have to worry, Knife Daddy." I wink at him.

Just then, the screams and rustling stop. I turn back around to see that Chris' body has gone limp, his eyes vacantly staring into nothingness.

"He lasted longer than I thought." AK chuckles as he pulls Chris off the hook.

"Why do you call him Knife Daddy?" Echo whispers as AK snatches the gasoline can from the floor and begins emptying the contents on the ground around Chris' body.

"Oh, Little Spark, that's a story for another day. Can we get you out of here?" I hold out my hand to her in question.

It takes several moments before she makes a move to decide one way or the other, and after several painfully long breaths, she places her hand in mine. I physically relax at the feel of her skin on mine, leading her out of the room and up the stairs. We pass back by all the impressive features I had been in awe of on the way in.

"Do you know if anyone else is here?" I arch a brow at her as I look up the grand staircase.

"Not anymore. He never let anyone else come here. It was only one of them at a time." The statement cuts off in her throat before I meet her gaze. Her green eyes that have seen so much cut through me as she searches for her next words. "Unless they're having a party... with us."

My blood begins to boil at her admission.

"Those cock-sucking motherfuckers!" I snarl. "I will end them for you, Little Spark."

I squeeze her hand in mine in an attempt to reassure her.

I know her. I *know* that I know her. Only one person has ever called me 'Little Spark', but there's no way that she could have grown up to be the woman in front of me. I shake the thought from my head as she leads me to the door. The sound of footsteps padding toward us makes me freeze.

"It's ok, Sunshine. It's just me." AK's velvety voice comes from behind me. "Keep moving. I'm coming up behind you with the rest of the trail."

Pocket's grip tightens around my hand as she drags me from the mansion toward a blacked-out van. I freeze, stopping dead in my tracks at the sight.

"Please don't make me get in there," I whimper.

"Hey, Little Spark, it's ok. You can sit up front if you're ok with AK driving." She turns to me, caressing my cheek with her hand in a sweet gesture that seems so unlike the blood thirsty woman I saw in that basement. "I promise you; he won't touch you."

I climb into the front seat, staring out the windshield, waiting for AK to return. I see him racing toward the van as smoke and the most beautiful mixture of red, orange, and yellow starts to illuminate the backdrop behind him. My eyes widen when I realize the house is engulfed in flames.

"Oh my god!" I barely recognize the scream coming from my lungs. "He's gonna get hurt!"

I raise my hands to my face, covering my eyes, so I don't have to witness the fire consume one of my saviors. I barely register when the driver-side door of the van opens.

"Hey Sunshine, it's ok." His sweet voice pulls me from the downward spiral of my mind.

"Oh my god, I thought you were going to die," I cry, before whispering, "because of me." My body begins to shake as sobs wrack through my body.

The drive leading away from the only home I've known in so long goes by quickly. I stare blankly at my hands, not paying attention to my surroundings, knowing no matter where the house was, I never wanted to return. I'm lost in my thoughts and memories when I realize the van has stopped. Probably has been for a while with the way I can feel AK and Pocket staring at me.

"Where are we?" I ask, raising my gaze to see a beautiful, brick building, the huge structure boasting large windows spread throughout the side facing us. It looks like an old factory.

"My place, or well, our place now." Pocket rolls her eyes as she lets her gaze trail down AK's towering form before she continues with an explanation, "They converted it into apartments a few years ago."

AK's out of the van without a word, stopping at the back to let Pocket out. Before I have a chance to act, he's at my door, opening it for me.

"Would you like a hand, Sunshine?" His kindness is something I haven't experienced from the opposite gender since before I was taken.

I shake my head, not ready to touch any part of any man. I step down and immediately gravitate toward Pocket, who is waiting several paces away. She holds out her hand in an offering, and it takes several beats before I make the decision to place my hand in hers again. She leads me to the front door of the old, converted factory, a steep staircase greeting us as we pass through the door. I instantly freeze at the sight, memories of a similarly steep staircase flashing through my mind.

"It's ok, my place is upstairs." Pocket's voice is so soft in her attempt to reassure me.

"I —" I start, unable to finish my thought as fear anchors me in place. I just keep my eyes trained on her icy-blue orbs.

"How about this," she offers, sliding her hand into her boot, pulling out the blade I used on Chris earlier. She presses the button to expose the blade before handing it to me, handle first. "If you feel threatened, now you have protection."

I don't know how to respond other than to take the weapon, holding it tentatively between my fingers. It's lighter than I expected, and the slim handle fits perfectly in my petite grip. I know I may not have any skills, but this may give me an illusion of safety to get through the next steps of whatever they've got planned for me.

"Trust me, Little Spark?" Her question along with her outstretched hand has flashes of Aladdin and Princess Jasmine going through my mind.

I pause for a moment, as more memories start to unfold. There's no way this is real. I place my hand in hers before Pocket leads me up the stairs. When we reach the door, she doesn't drop my hand, instead using her free one to enter a code into the digitally locked deadbolt. I do a double take. No, that couldn't have been what I thought... right?

Before I can think about it any further, Pocket opens the door with a quick turn of the knob, revealing a spacious room just inside. There is a dark plush couch up against the wall far, more modern than what I've become accustomed to. The exposed brick is beautiful, but it has an industrial feel that causes my stomach to twist, unsure what I've gotten myself into. I notice a TV close to the door and a laptop thrown on the couch as if they left in the middle of using it.

While admiring their home, I notice a presence behind me and spin on my heel, holding the knife in front of me to find myself face-to-face with AK. Well, face-to-chest really. The man is a giant in comparison to my five-foot-two frame.

"Whoa, Sunshine," he gasps, holding his hands up in surrender. "I'm not going to hurt you. Even if I wanted to, which I don't"—he nods toward Pocket—"she'd have my balls, and I'd much rather they stay in place."

I can't help the giggle that passes my lips, which surprises me. He's the first man who has spoken to me like an actual human being, and not just a means to his own pleasure.

"Come on, let me show you around and then we can all get cleaned up." Pocket comes between AK and me, pressing her hand lightly against his chest as she laces her fingers with mine.

# thirteen
# ECHO

The hot water cascades down my naked body, the yellow and purple bruises littering my skin a mocking reminder of where I'd been. They're healing pretty well, considering just how badly Chris beat me this time. I smirk to myself as the dried blood from his final moments tinges the water pink as I wash away the past twelve years.

Tears begin to fall as I stand under the scalding stream, reality finally sinking in. *I'm free; I'm finally free.* I breathe a sigh of relief at the realization.

The solace is short lived, though, as I begin to second guess leaving with Pocket and AK. *I left one hell, following them blindly. What if this is worse?* I feel my body tense as sobs begin to wrack through me.

Memories of my childhood, from before I was taken, flash through my mind. Her blonde curls bouncing as she chased after us; Chloe was her sister's shadow. There was never a day that that sweet girl wasn't with us. She could never hurt me. Not like they have.

Long after the water has run cold, I step out, grabbing the towel that Pocket gave me before she left. I wrap it around myself before stepping in front of the vanity. Taking a moment to look in the mirror for the first time since they took me, I gaze at my reflection, really taking in just how abused my body actually looks.

I know it will heal in time, but it's still jarring to see. I've always felt the bruises when Chris and the others who came around would beat us. Seeing them on her was one thing... but seeing the injuries scattered across my own skin has a fresh round of tears filling my eyes, and a shock wave of emotion reverberates through me. At least my best friend never had to see herself like this.

After I'm not even sure how much time has passed, I dress in the sweatpants and band t-shirt that was left for me. They're huge on my tiny frame, and I have to roll the waistband down multiple times just to keep them up, and I'm still stepping on them as I walk out of the room. Pocket greets me with a warm smile, and AK's eyes meet mine for a brief moment, taking in my outfit before he smirks and turns away.

"Would you like anything to eat?" Pocket's offer has AK cocking a brow at her.

"You never ask me if I'm hungry," he taunts her.

"Because whenever I make something, I assume you're hungry and make enough for you too." She rolls her eyes at him.

"Aw, you do care, Killer." He bats his eyelashes at her, and I find myself smiling at the funny way he teases her.

"Shut up." She doesn't bother hiding her grin.

I enjoy watching their back and forth. It's adorable, and I'm so glad she's found someone who is so good to her. She deserves that.

"May I have some soup, please?" I ask quietly.

"Of course, Little Spark. Do you still like chicken dumpling soup?" The memory of my grandmother cooking that for the three of us makes my heart ache in my chest.

I nod at her, taking a few moments to gather my thoughts, then I take a few steps closer to where she stands in the kitchen, her eyes locked on me.

"It's really you, isn't it?" My voice shakes with the question. I'm unsure if I actually want to hear the answer.

"Yea. We can talk about it later. There's a lot we need to discuss, Little Spark." She pauses briefly as she glances at AK. "Just, not yet."

I nod again, staring down at my hands as I push the memories from my mind. I'm not ready to relive them. I can't do this right now. I can't go back there. I can't remember what it was like before. I can't allow myself to show any weakness. Not now, not ever. Weakness makes it worse.

"Hey, Sunshine." AK's voice startles me out of my thoughts. I raise my gaze to meet his beautiful face etched with concern. "You're safe here. I promise you that. I know you don't know me but believe me when I say I will end anyone who tries to come near you with ill intent." He shoots a loving look to Pocket. "Near either of you."

The way he growls the declaration sends chills through me. I can't remember the last time a man was so kind to me. They've used me in such painful ways solely for their pleasure. It makes my chest tighten, but this time I don't recognize the feeling that's behind it. It's foreign and feels funny.

Before I have a chance to think deeper on my emotions, Pocket places a bowl of soup on the island bar next to where AK is sitting. I suck in a deep breath before taking a step closer.

"I'll go hang out on the couch with my headphones, so you two can talk." He gets up from his bar stool, shooting me a smile that steals my breath.

"Get the fuck out of here with that. You can't turn that smile on her until she has time to heal and process, asshole." Pocket throws a roll at his head which he dodges easily.

"It's just my smile!" He chuckles with a sly smirk. Oh, he knows exactly what he's doing.

AK disappears behind us. I glance up after a moment of silence, Pocket looking over my shoulder, to see him sitting on the couch with his feet on the coffee table, and a pair of big, bright, candy-apple red headphones covering his ears.

"I haven't gone by the name you remember me by since I left." Pocket's voice has me turning back around in my seat.

"Why?" I ask as I drag a spoonful of soup to my lips.

Mmm.

The appreciative moan erupts from my throat before I realize what I've done. My face tinges pink in embarrassment.

"This tastes just like grandma's, Chl—Pocket." I catch myself from using her former name at the last second.

She smiles and nods in understanding. "It should, Little Spark, it's her recipe. She was the only adult I knew I could trust."

"What happened? Why did you leave?" I can't help questioning her. I don't want to talk about me, and from what I remember of her, she will push me for information.

Her eyes turn sad, and she looks down, avoiding my eyes for several minutes.

"My parents sold Ivy. They wanted to get rid of me, but whoever they sold her to knew I had been experimenting..." The words die on her tongue. "Apparently I wasn't clean enough for him."

I cover my mouth, gasping at her words.

"Oh, my god... You've been looking for her? This whole time?" Tears start streaming down my face.

"Every day since I turned eighteen." She offers me a weak smile. "I started training immediately when I realized they weren't going to save her."

I can't tell her. She'll never forgive me.

I drop my gaze to my bowl of soup. The thought of eating now making me want to vomit. The smell wafts into my nose, mocking me, daring me to eat. But I can't, not when the truth she needs to hear sits so heavily in my gut.

I wake, my blankets soaked through. With a shiver, I sit up, looking around. I'm still on their couch. I'm still here. I'm still safe.

A week has passed since they found me. I've told Pocket and AK most of what they did to us, but I haven't told her who my other half was. She's tried to push, but I always shut down. I'm not ready to lose her, too. I don't even know if my grandma is still alive. Even if she is, would she want to see me? Would I be able to handle seeing her? My thoughts continue to spiral, my breaths coming in short bursts before the sound of AK's voice shakes me free.

"Sunshine?" AK whispers as he stalks toward me in the dark. "Are you ok?"

I sigh heavily in defeat. "It was another nightmare. When will they end?"

"I'm not sure, but we'll help you get through it. Do you need anything or just a change of blankets?" This sweet smile is so unlike what I've come to expect from him, and I find it leaves a strange feeling in my tummy.

"Just blankets, thank you." I still haven't found it in myself to hold his eye contact for more than a second. He's got the kindest heart; I've seen how he is with Pocket. Their relationship is so beautiful it's almost sickening. He disappears into the bedroom again for a few moments before returning with new blankets to replace the sweat-soaked mess currently covering me.

If I'm honest, I'm jealous. I never expected Pocket to end up with a man. It always seemed like she was interested in women. *Only* women. But maybe I was wrong. I shrug at the memories of her from my youth. She was never mine, so it shouldn't matter. I just want her to be happy, and he makes her happy.

"Thank you," I say as he helps me change the bedding. He just nods in acknowledgment, taking the soaked items to the laundry basket in the bathroom.

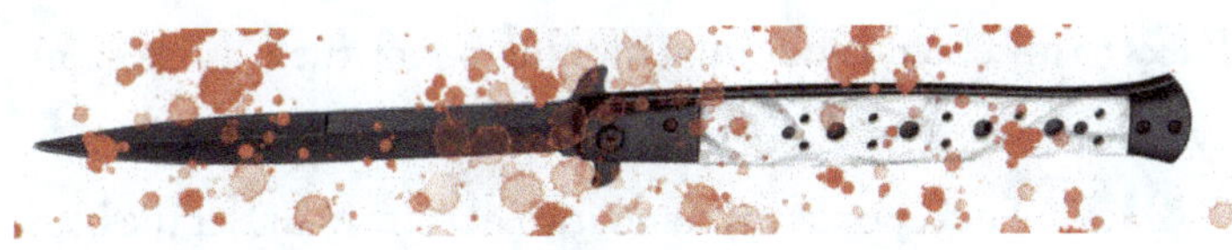

"Killer? Sunshine?" I hear AK call for us from the bedroom. We've been up watching old episodes of *Buffy the Vampire Slayer* like we used to as kids.

"Out here, Knife Daddy!" Pocket calls him to the living room where we're snuggled up on the couch together.

Over the past few weeks, Pocket and I have been getting closer, falling easily into the friendship we had as kids. I was tossing and turning one night on the couch, and she couldn't sleep, so she came out and turned on Buffy. We've made it a point to watch at least two episodes a night since. Right now, Buffy and the gang are fighting against Ethan, who has created a candy bar to make adults relive their youth to abduct the infants of the town. Ethan was a real motherfucker.

"I hate him," AK says as he sits down on the other side of Pocket.

"Wait, you watched Buffy too?" Pocket and I say in unison. I'm unable to hide the excitement from my voice, while Pocket stares at him with a brow arched in disbelief.

"Only a monster wouldn't watch Buffy." He shrugs.

"Damn, you just got even hotter." Pocket laughs as she presses her chest against his, turning away from me.

I sit up, pulling the blanket up higher over myself, tucking my knees to my chest, and resting my chin on my them as I keep my eyes on the screen.

"Hey?" Pocket pulls my hand into hers from under the blanket. "Why did you move?"

"I didn't want to intrude now that he's here. It's ok." I smile weakly at her, my eyes darting to AK before returning to her beautiful face.

"Little Spark, you're not intruding on anything. I want you here, too." She swipes her thumb over my palm.

I gasp at the shock of heat that jolts through me from her touch.

"I— I—" The words die on my lips as I stand from my place on the couch and rush out of the apartment, the blanket tangling around my feet, nearly taking me out in the process.

Not that I have anywhere to go. I quickly make it down the stairs to the main door of the building. Pushing the heavy barrier to the outside world open and being enveloped by the fresh air allows me to breathe more easily. It's not that it has been my first time outside since they found me; however, it is the first time I've been outside alone.

Taking a seat on the steps, I pull my knees into my chest. Terror radiates through me as I think about what she could have meant by her words. Her touch. It was too intimate to not be insinuating something. Was she really suggesting I be with her in front of him? Or both of them? I—

My thoughts are cut short by a throat clearing behind me.

"Sunshine?" AK's smooth voice wraps around me in the cool evening air like a security blanket I didn't realize I crave.

"I'm ok; I just need a minute," I lie. I am not ok. Not by a long shot.

"Sunshine, you know what I do for a living, right?" He sits down next to me. I can hear the amusement in his voice.

"I don't know exactly. I just assume that you and Pocket..." I don't finish my thought.

"I get paid to take out bad people. The worst kind of assholes, which is how I ended up finding Pocket. We both were after the same man." He leans against my side; his body is so warm it almost makes me want the cool breeze to come back. "Because of what I do, I've been forced to become a master human lie detector."

I sigh, knowing he can see right through me. "Ok, Fine, I'm not ok. I don't know what came over me. But I'll be fine, really," I lie again. I can't help it. I can't admit where my mind went. He'll think I'm crazy.

He chuckles so softly to himself I barely hear him.

"I'm going to tell you what I think," he pauses, allowing me time to process. "I think she is attracted to you and, as subtly as she knows how, came on to you. I think it scared you. I think you are out here beating yourself up because of my relationship with her."

"I—I—wh—what?" I stutter over my words. Am I really that transparent?

"Mmhmm," he mumbles as he smirks at me.

We sit there for a while without a word passing between us. It's strange that he understands me so deeply when I've tried to avoid him at all costs. At least before tonight.

"If it helps settle your nerves, I don't need to be around if you make the decision to be with her." He is sure to enunciate the word 'you'. "It's her body, and it's her choice to add someone to the mix. I'm just along for the ride. Quite literally." He winks at me.

My face heats at his insinuation. As attracted as I am to her, I don't know if I'm ready to bare myself to anyone yet. Sure, every day that passes has been better than the last, and the nightmares are further between in recent days, but I've never even been with someone willingly.

I've been watching the two of them since we brought Echo back here. Whether or not my Killer realizes it, she's been giving off long-lost love vibes since she realized who Echo actually was. It's been adorable. She may know how to disembowel a person in one swift move, but damn is she smitten over this little ray of sunshine. After telling Echo to take her time to process our conversation and that I'd keep Pocket distracted for a while, I head back upstairs.

I step inside the front door of Pocket's apartment again to see her sitting on the couch looking like Shonda Rhimes just killed off her favorite character. Don't judge me, ok? I have sisters. I cross the apartment, so I'm standing in front of her.

"Beautiful, she'll come around, give her some more time." I smirk at her. My eyes roaming the length of her body. "Do you want to watch another episode without her, or do you want to come back to bed, and I can take your mind off of things?"

She watches the door for a few moments before letting out a heavy sigh. "It's not the same watching without her. Did you tell her we're going to bed?" She turns off the TV and stands, closing the distance between us.

"I told her a lot of things, but yes that was one of them. Now, come on." I lean down pressing a light kiss against her lips before lifting her into my arms, her perfectly muscular ass filling my hands as her legs wrap around my waist.

"Knife Daddy," she whimpers as she digs her nails into my scalp, trying to pull my mouth back to hers. "Let's go to the shower, I want you to fill me with your cock of steel and fuck my ass with Ursula. I need to feel the blade digging into my ass when you fill my pussy."

"You poor unfortunate soul or, I guess, you'll be a full unfortunate soul when I'm done with you." I chuckle darkly as I cross the room in just a few long strides, tossing her on the bed.

"But I want you to—" The words are cut off when I tear her black spider print sleep shorts from her body. Honestly, they're a terrible excuse for coverage, her ass is hanging out of them. I could feel how wet she was when I lifted her into my arms just from the brief swipe of my fingers along her core.

"You're going to let me have the snack I woke up for, Killer. I haven't tasted you for too fucking long." My lips twitch as I see her processing my words.

"It's been like five—" Her words are lost as I dip my tongue between her folds, swiping up her length, bringing her arousal up to her clit.

"Oh, god, yes!" she cries out softy.

"Killer, you can do better than that." A dark chuckle rumbles from my throat again. "How about I make it interesting?" Arching a brow at her, I swipe my tongue against her clit one last time before I stand. She whimpers almost inaudibly. She's been trying so hard to be quiet because of Echo's presence in the apartment, but that stops tonight.

I step around the bed to grab Ursula from her nightstand. I find it immediately since it's become her favorite and one of our more frequently used toys. Well, it had been until Echo arrived. Pocket loses all control when this thing touches her. I lift the teal, purple, and coral-colored tentacle vibrator into the light. Glancing back at her, I see her hands stroking her pussy. My eyes meet hers when she sees Ursula.

"Fuck! Knife Daddy, please!" She sobs as her hands continue spreading her arousal around her clit.

"Oh, Killer, please what?" I smirk at her.

"Please, I need you. I'll give you what you want. Please." She attempts to sit, reaching for me as I make my way back to where she's sprawled out.

"It's cute that you think there was ever another option." Dropping to my knees in front of her again, I swirl my tongue in tight circles around her clit as I slide the tentacle inside her cunt so slowly her hips buck off the bed begging for more. Once it's fully seated inside her perfect little hole, I press the power button, and Ursula comes to life inside her.

"Oh, Jesus Christ, Knife Daddy. Please!" Her cries of pleasure have me fisting my cock as I latch onto her clit, sucking it between my lips while I thrust the wildly moving vibrator in and out of her cunt.

Pre-cum leaks from the tip of my dick as I pump myself, working to bring her closer to her release. Her hips meet me with every thrust of the tentacle, her cries and whimpers growing louder and louder with every twist of the vibrator. I graze my teeth over her clit lightly before swirling my tongue around it again.

"Oh, god, I'm so fucking close!" she screams for me.

I increase the vibration on Ursula while I suck her clit between my lips again, harder than before, which sets her off. She detonates around the toy and screams out an unintelligible string of words as pleasure takes over. I continue fucking her with Ursula for several more moments as she comes down from her high before turning it off and laying Ursula on the bed next to us before I crawl up her body.

"Such a good girl." I smirk at her, pressing a kiss against her lips as she pants, her breathing still ragged from her orgasm. "Next time, don't fight me on it. I'll always give you what you want, Beautiful." I wink at her before swiping my tongue against hers and rolling onto my back, stroking myself. My dick still hard as stone.

I can tell the moment she hears noises from the living room. Her eyes go wide and a bright smile spreads across her face.

"Have fun, Killer." I chuckle as she slides off the bed and quietly sneaks out of the room.

I walk back into the living room only a few moments after AK left me to my own thoughts. He's right. I am scared. I'm fucking terrified. For the first time, I actually want someone. I mean she's gorgeous. How could I not want her? She is a goddess, putting Aphrodite to shame. As promised, the room is empty, and I'm left alone once again.

I lie on the couch, staring at the ceiling, thinking about what I want. What can I truly offer her when I don't even know how to take care of myself? I groan as I roll onto my side, burying my face into the back of the couch, trying to force my brain to make a decision when I hear a noise that I can't place.

I roll onto my back, listening for the sound again. It takes a couple of moments before I hear it, but there's no mistaking it's Pocket and AK. Well, it sounds like mostly Pocket. I strain to hear more clearly and hear her cry out.

"Fuck! Knife Daddy, please!" The desire and need in her voice send a rush of heat to my core that I've only felt a few times in my life, all since I've been here with the two of them.

I can make out her pleas as she begs him for more. It's so goddamn sexy, and I press my thighs together, hoping the pressure will make the strange ache I'm feeling between my legs lessen. Newsflash: it only makes it worse. I softly groan at the frustration of my current predicament.

"Oh, Jesus Christ, Knife Daddy. Please!" Pocket is even louder now, and it's as if the door is wide open, even though glancing to my right, I can see it's still closed.

Several moments later, the excruciatingly perfect sounds become too much. I slip my hand under the waistband of my pink polka-dot sleep shorts and the thin white cotton panties Pocket bought for me. When I reach my pussy, I feel a damp heat I'm not used to. Dipping my fingers between my lips to reach the ache, I gasp when I find myself soaking wet. For a moment, I worry I got my period, but this feels different. I slide my fingers through the slickness, dragging it up to the most sensitive spot I've ever felt on my body.

A soft whimper escapes my lip as I press my fingers against the bundle of nerves. I swirl my fingers around my clit, the throbbing ache intensifying in the most glorious way. Oh, my god.

"Oh, god, I'm so fucking close."

Pocket's cries from the other room have a tingling sensation shooting straight to that sensitive bud, which is begging for more attention.

I rub tight circles as soft moans pass my lips. Unable to stop myself, I cry out as the most intense feeling I've ever experienced rips through my body. I squeeze my eyes shut, my core tightening as I imagine Pocket standing in front of me, her hands in place of mine.

"Oh, god," I sob quietly into the empty room.

"Little Spark?" My eyes shoot open, my face immediately heating with embarrassment as I take in Pocket standing bare before me.

"Oh, my god, I'm so sorry." I yank my hand from my shorts and sit up, curling myself into a tight ball in the corner of the couch.

"Oh, no! Little Spark, you've got it all wrong." She smiles gently at me. "Do you trust me?"

I raise my head from my knees, glancing up to meet her heated gaze.

"Yes," I say immediately.

"I'm not going to do anything you don't want me to. You can tell me no, ok?" She looks more nervous than I've ever seen her, a vulnerability that seems out of place from her usually confident demeanor.

"Ok?" I ask her as I begin to relax knowing she's not mad at me.

"May I kiss you?" The question is a whisper, but she may as well have shouted it from the rooftops.

I stare at her, unable to breathe for a moment before nodding my head.

"Echo, use your words. I'm not going to touch you unless you tell me I can, understand?" She sounds calm but the edge in her voice tells me she needs this as much as I do.

"Yes," I breathe.

As soon as the word passes my lips, she's on her knees, kneeling next to me on the couch. Her soft lips press gently against my mouth, and she tangles her fingers into my mane of sandy colored hair.

Her mouth expertly moves against mine, and when I feel her tongue swipe against my bottom lip, a gasp escapes me. She takes that as an invitation, exploring my mouth. The way she flicks and glides her tongue in an experienced lashing against my own has me writhing in my seat. I raise my hands to her hair, digging my fingers into her vibrant blue locks, holding on for dear life as she opens my eyes to an experience I never thought I'd have. She slowly ends the kiss, both of us panting after the exchange.

"Goddamn, Echo." She smirks at me, her lips twitching as she mulls over something in her head.

"That was... wow." I giggle pressing my forehead against hers.

"Echo," She lifts my chin so that my eyes are on hers. With her other hand, she lifts my hand that was in my pants and brings it to her lips, sucking the digit into her mouth. A soft moan escapes Pocket's lips as her tongue swirls around, making sure she tastes all of me before she continues. "You taste so fucking good. May I?"

"You just did?" I'm so unsure of what she's asking.

"Oh, Little Spark, that's not enough." She grins as she lowers a hand and quickly swipes a finger over the damp patch of my sleep shorts.

A whimper passes my lips I wasn't prepared for. A noise I've never made before. Why did that feel so good?

"Why would you want to taste me?" I ask shyly.

"Oh, Little Spark, you have so much to learn." The devilish smirk that forms on her lips catches me off guard.

She swipes a finger over my panties again as if to taunt me. I need this. I need her.

"Ok," I whisper.

"I need a yes or no, gorgeous." Pocket's face softens.

"Yes." It's barely a breath, but she hears it, and her grin turns into something predatory.

She drops to the floor, kneeling between my legs before she digs her fingers into the band of my sleep shorts, tugging them down as if getting me bare is more important than her next breath. I lift my hips, allowing her to drag the shorts and panties over my hips and down my legs before she tosses them on the floor somewhere behind her. Immediately, I squeeze my legs together, unsure if I'm ready for her to see me this close. She notices my hesitation and pauses, looking up at me.

"Hey, you say the word, and I stop, ok? I may want to make you feel as amazing as a person can feel, but I will not push you. You got me?" She cocks a brow, expecting a response.

"Yes, I got you, but they — they did things to me." The confession leaves me in a rush.

"They can't hurt you anymore, Little Spark." She raises my left foot, pressing a soft kiss against the arch, nipping the skin gently before resting it on her shoulder. I gasp at her sensual touch, which has a softness that is such a drastic contrast to the roughness I've become accustomed to. Fuck, that feels good.

She repeats the pattern, guiding herself up to my ankle, calf, and thigh. I can feel a pulse between my legs that wasn't this noticeable before. When I think she's going to come face to face with my pussy, she bends my leg and places my foot on the couch so I'm partially squatting. Before I have a chance to ask what she's doing she brings my other leg to her shoulder and goes through the same process. My skin is on fire, heated with a need I've never felt before.

"Pl—please, P—Pock—et," I stutter out.

"Please, what?" She smirks at me as she bends the leg she has in her grasp and places this foot on the couch cushion as well, leaving me in a seated squat, my legs spread, baring myself to her, but she hasn't looked down to see me.

"I ne—need you," I cry as she drags her nails up my thighs so achingly slow that I think I may explode from the anticipation.

"You're going to keep your eyes on me, Little Spark. You take your eyes away, and I stop. Understood?" She leans down and swipes her tongue against my thigh.

"Oh, god, yes. I understand." I'm whimpering with a need I've never experienced in my life.

"Good girl." She smiles wickedly before she dips her face between my thighs again, this time, the nips and licks don't stop until she reaches my pussy lips. Her eyes still locked on mine as she nips and sucks them between her lips so gently, I'm bucking into her face. My head rolls back at the sensation and then just as quickly as she had me on cloud nine, she's gone.

"Eyes. On. Me," she scolds, a wild smile on her lips that makes a fresh wave of arousal rush to my core.

I lock my eyes on her again. This time as her face disappears between my thighs, I feel her tongue swipe the length of my folds. I sob in frustration. She giggles as she wraps her arms around my ankles and thighs. I usually hate being held after everything but not here, now, with her. The desire to submit to anything she asks of me is overwhelming.

My eyes remain locked on Pocket as she finally flicks her tongue against my clit. I groan, needing more. I lift my hands from my sides, tangling my fingers in her beautiful blue hair. I feel the grin against my skin as she continues her sensual assault against the sensitive bundle of nerves. The way she can go from a vicious killer covered in blood to the angelic sight she is on her knees before me sends a jolt of pleasure through me. My Angel.

I cry out as she picks up speed, swirling her tongue in tight circles around my clit, flicking and sucking all in a staccato rhythm that has me shaking. My limbs trembling as she works the most amazing explosion of sensation from me.

"Oh, god. Please. Oh, fuck," I cry out, grinding against her face, my head rolling back as I fall over a cliff of pleasure. My chest heaves as I slowly come back down to earth several long moments later. I untangle my fingers from her hair one at a time, and before she pulls away, I feel a smirk against my skin as she swipes my clit one last time, making me arch into her.

"Such a good girl, my Little Spark." The pride on her face makes my heart swell.

"Thank you, Angel," I murmur as I fall back onto the couch, stretching my legs out in front of me before she slips onto the cushion, lying beside me. I attempt to move my hand to touch her, but she stops me, lifting my hand to her lips to lessen the sting.

"Not tonight sweet girl, this was about you." She presses her mouth against mine, swiping her tongue against my lips asking for entry again. I oblige' hell, I'd sell a kidney on the black market right now if she asked me to. Her tongue sweeps inside my mouth, tangling with mine as a sweet, yet tangy flavor explodes on my taste buds. I stiffen for a brief moment when I realize it's me that I taste, before melting into her, enjoying every moment of the closeness she's offering me right now. But a seed of doubt still lingers in the back of my mind.

*This can't last forever, can it?*

Echo is still lying snug against me, her arm draped over my stomach. I wrap my arms around her waist, holding her close as I open my eyes. I glance toward my bedroom to see AK leaning against the door frame, watching us like the creep he is. He has a sly smile on his face like he's proud of himself. Though, I'm not going to lie. He did kind of make this happen, and I'm glad. Between the earth-shattering orgasm he gave me and the life-changing climax for Echo, it was a great night.

I mouth good morning before nodding at him to go back into the room. He chuckles, shaking his head before disappearing back into my space. I feel a heat in my core I'm all too familiar with; between having AK around and Echo's reappearance into my life, I've been living in a constant state of arousal. I gently roll her onto her back as I silently snake down her body, my hands roaming the contours of her gorgeous form.

I smile when I realize she fell asleep without putting on her shorts or panties. In the harsh light of day, I see what she was hiding last night. It looks like her thighs and the skin around her pussy were sliced with multiple knives over the years. None look incredibly recent, but it's obvious they took joy in torturing her this way.

I make a note to find out the names of anyone who has ever touched her. I'll fucking end them.

I press my lips against each scar, swiping my tongue along the length of every faded injury. I will make her fall in love with them; these marks show what a goddamn warrior she is.

She begins to stir, and I stop, not ready for her to wake just yet. Once she settles back into sleep, I dip my tongue between her folds, tasting her arousal. I've barely even started, and she's soaking like the needy Little Spark that she is. Smiling against her skin, I continue slow, sensual, and deliberate swipes of my tongue up the length as my hands roam up to her waist. I dig my fingers into her hips, holding onto her. When I have a good enough hold, I begin the real feast. Flicking, swirling, and sucking on her clit until she's writhing beneath me. She awakes, whimpering until she realizes it's me. The moment her eyes fly open and she meets my wicked gaze, she lets go of any semblance of subtlety and cries out, my name on her lips.

"Oh, god, Pocket, please!" she cries out as the pleasure pulls her out of the haze of unconsciousness.

I feel a fresh wave of arousal drench my tongue as her body trembles. She reaches her crescendo, and I smile up at her, pressing a soft kiss against her thigh.

"Good morning, Little Spark. Mind if I try something more?"

"I? Sure." She doesn't fight me as her chest heaves, coming down slowly from her high.

Before she gets a chance to fully recover, I pull her clit between my lips once more, paying close attention to the spot I know she enjoys most. I alternate between flicking my tongue and swirling a pleasant mixture of her arousal and my saliva around her sensitive bundle of nerves. She's sobbing again as the pleasure begins to build back up. With my eyes locked on her face, I slide a finger inside her tight channel. She stiffens for a fraction of a second when she realizes what I'm doing but quickly relaxes back into my touch as my tongue works her over. I pump my long digit inside her a few times before adding another. This time she doesn't stiffen but moans louder with an air of excitement around her she didn't have earlier.

"Oh god, oh god, oh god." She whimpers as she begins to meet me thrust for thrust. Curling my fingers, I find her g-spot. Stroking the most sensitive part of her body, I drag another orgasm from her. This time around, I can tell she's more awake as soon as her hands land in my hair again, tangling the blue strands around her fingers as she holds me firmly in place, riding my face until an orgasm crashes through her like a tsunami. It floods my mouth as her body trembles under me. I giggle to myself when I see the blissed-out expression on her face. I dip my tongue between her folds one more time ready to bring her to the brink of ecstasy, enjoying her pleasure even more than my own when she cries out, "Stop."

I pull my fingers from her pussy and sit up, immediately pulling her to me.

"Little Spark"—I try to read the expression on her face—"what did I do?"

"You're trying to kill me by orgasms, aren't you?" She smirks at me from under her dark lashes. "You didn't do anything, but I'm pretty sure if I come again, I'm going to pass out."

"You had me worried." I giggle and pull her into my arms, pressing a soft kiss against her hair.

I hear a throat clear in the other room.

"Do you mind if he comes out?" I ask, my arms still wrapped tightly around her.

She nods so subtly I barely notice it. I release her for just a second, pulling the blanket around her waist before responding.

"Come on out, perv," I sass as AK appears in the doorway again.

"Killer, Sunshine, that was hot as fuck. But if you don't want me to listen, keep it down next time." He winks and her face flushes in embarrassment.

AK closes the distance between us, bending to press his lips against mine. When he tastes her, he deepens the kiss, swiping his tongue inside to get every last drop from me. I moan into him, digging my nails into his scalp, enjoying the tongue lashing he's giving me. He breaks the kiss after a moment and turns to Echo.

"You taste delicious, Sunshine," he says, flashing her that goddamn panty dropping grin.

"Oh, my god." She covers her face with her hands as she shrinks back into the couch.

AK chuckles, enjoying the torment he's causing because she's not running away like she would have in the beginning. I squirm in the seat next to Echo, sliding my hand under the blanket and squeezing her thigh.

She lowers her hands, her eyes meeting mine, and I lean forward, pressing my lips against hers. She melts into me for a moment before pushing me away. I gasp when I realize what she's doing. Echo climbs her way up my body as I lie back on the couch. A mischievous grin spreads on her face as she presses feather-light kisses up my body, then lifts my shirt up over my breasts, exposing me to the room. I hear an audible groan from AK. I grin as I see him palm himself in my periphery.

I let out my own whimper as Echo latches onto my bare breast, sucking and licking my nipple while palming my other so gently it's almost unbearable. I'm not used to being handled with care. Although, with her, it feels kind of perfect. Her hands travel down my curves until she reaches the waistband of my panties.

"Little Spark, you don't have to do this," I assure her, trying to be respectful of her healing process even if I need to come like a motherfucker. She releases my nipple with a pop as she glances up at me.

"Shut up, Angel." She smirks. "I know you won't make me do anything I don't want to, which is why I want to do this, why I need to."

She presses slow, wet kisses down my abdomen until she reaches the delicate skin just above my pussy. *I've never been so happy to be naked in my life.* I throw my head back against the cushions as she lets out a gentle breath against my center. I raise onto my elbows to watch her, and it's the most beautiful sight I've ever seen. Her mouth disappears between my thighs, her eyes closing as she connects with my aching mound. The instant her tongue touches me, my skin alights with a heat I've only felt with one other person. It's so intense, I cry out into the room. Her tongue moves expertly around my clit, manipulating my body to her will.

"Jesus Christ, fuck!" I scream.

How has she never done this before?

She spreads my pussy apart with one hand, allowing the other to continue rubbing tight circles around my clit while she lowers herself. She spears me with her long tongue, repeatedly thrusting in and out of me until my legs are trembling. As soon as she feels my pussy tighten around her tongue, she flicks inside of me several times before lapping up the arousal that has escaped.

"Holy fuck, how—" I don't even get the question out before her mouth is on me again, sending me over the edge for a second time after just a few moments.

I feel the bed dip as Echo climbs in on the other side of Pocket and open my eyes, taking in the sight before me. Fuck, my Sunshine is everything light and beautiful with the world, while my Killer is every perfect shadow in the darkness. She may not realize it yet, but she's mine, just as much as Pocket is.

"Hey Sunshine," I say, my voice gravely with sleep. "What are you doing up so early?" I glance at the clock noticing it's only three A.M.

"I had a nightmare. I didn't want to wake you two, so I just slipped out and sat outside for a bit to clear my head." Her voice is quiet. Too quiet. She's terrified.

"You want to come lay with me?" I ask, arching a brow.

She may not have let me inside her yet, but she's been warming up to me over the past couple of weeks since Pocket broke through her walls. Echo crawls over Pocket and slides in between us. I roll onto my side as she spoons our girl and wrap my arm around them both.

"Thank you, Knife Daddy." Echo's sweetness with the name that my Killer calls me has me groaning as my cock hardens against her ass.

"Sunshine," I growl into her hair. "Behave. A man can only handle so much. Especially with as often as I've had to witness you two going at it."

She giggles and snuggles into Pocket while placing her hand over mine.

It only takes a few moments before I feel her steady breathing against my chest, and I know she's fallen asleep. I hate that she has been struggling so much with her nightmares. They may not be as often, but they sure as hell are just as intense when they happen. The rage I feel inside when I think about everything she's gone through... It makes me want to murder every motherfucker who has ever harmed her. I want her to get vengeance against all of those who have wronged her and the friend she has been too afraid to tell Pocket about. Though, I have a feeling I know why.

The thrall of unconsciousness calls back to me, pulling me under after the decision is made. I will help her end them. All of them.

"Killer," I say as I walk into the bathroom where Pocket is showering. She and Echo have been watching Buffy all fucking day. They're on the final season and don't want to stop until it's over.

I can see her beautiful curves through the glass doors, and she doesn't hear me over the running water. I lift my shirt over my head, and shuck my sweatpants down, stepping in behind her. I wrap my arms around her waist, and she lets out a what sounds like a shriek and a gasp rolled into one. She turns to face me, still caged in my arms.

"Knife Daddy, you scared the shit out of me. I thought you were staying out there and having lunch with Echo." The grin she gives tells me she's happy to have a moment alone with me.

"I missed you, and I wanted to run something by you." I smirk at her, and she melts into me.

"God damn, why do you have to have the body you do and have the ability to get whatever you want from me with just one fucking look," she whines.

My cock is hard against her belly, and she wraps her hand around it, playing with the piercings. I groan as I thrust into her grasp.

"Because you love me, Killer. Admit it, and I'll let you do something you haven't been able to since we've met." I run my tongue over my lips as I lower my face to her neck, running my nose up the column of her throat.

"Wh-what are you going to let me do?" The way I can affect her so completely makes my cock pulse against her abdomen.

I know she can feel it because she swallows hard at the same moment.

"I'll let you use me the way you used your old targets. Tie me up. Inject me with that instant-boner shit and treat me like a fuck doll for as long as you can go." My lips twitch the moment I see my words register in her mind.

"You, what? Really?" She stumbles over her words.

I chuckle darkly, knowing the initial inject-a-boner is going to hurt like a motherfucker, but I also know she needs to tell me.

"What about—" she pauses when I push her gently, pressing her against the wall of the shower.

I lift her up, her legs wrapping around my waist as I slide the head of my cock inside her.

"Go on, Killer. Ask what you need to." I grin down at her as I inch myself deeper inside.

She's panting at the intrusion. It's been at least twelve hours since I last filled her. Before Echo, we would fuck a few times a day. Now that she has another way to be sated, I have less time to feel her around me.

"Can she use you?" she gasps out as she looks off to the doorway where Echo is standing.

Her eyes are hooded with a lust-filled desire. I glance down and see her hand is slipped under her panties as she's leaning against the door frame, her eyes locked on me and Pocket.

Fuck.

I thrust into my Killer, filling her to the hilt, not allowing her any time to adjust. She lets out a beautiful yelp of ecstasy. Her nails dig into me, both of us watching Echo pleasure herself as she watches us fuck. I will be in so much fucking trouble when she lets me get my hands on her, too.

"Anything you two want to do to me," I say, my eyes still locked on my Sunshine for just a moment longer.

Turning my full attention back to Pocket, I take her chin between my fingers, forcing her eyes back to mine. I crash my lips against hers as I continue rutting into her. The whimpers and moans that escape from her mouth into mine have me growing even harder inside her. Plus, knowing that we have an audience has me ready to lose control way too soon. I glance back over to Echo who is softy whimpering as she comes undone around her own fingers. I groan as I thrust into Pocket again.

"Sunshine, get over here and put your hand between us. Make our girl come around my cock," I say as gently as I can, knowing this may be more than she bargained for when she made her way in here. I feel Pocket clench around me, her breath catching. I know she wants this as much as I do.

Echo's lips turn into a shy smile as she steps forward, opening the shower door and stepping inside to join us, still clad in my t-shirt and panties. She's not quite ready to fully bare herself to me, but that's ok. We'll get there.

She leans against the wall next to Pocket and reaches out and cups her neck, pulling my Killer's face to her, their mouths crash together as I continue taking my girl as hard as I can, knowing

I'm about to burst. Seeing them kissing up close like this is so much more intimate than what they've allowed me before. They are both so fucking beautiful.

Echo's hand slides around Pocket's side, snaking down her stomach until she reaches right between where Pocket and I are connected. Her fingers slide down, wrapping around me, and a guttural moan leaves my throat. I didn't fucking expect this. I thrust against both Echo and Pocket at once, my balls tightening, ready to explode.

With each thrust, Pocket cries out, and I realize that in the position our Sunshine is in, has her palm applying the perfect amount of friction to give Pocket what she needs. My movements become erratic as I reach my high, Pocket's pussy tightening around my cock as we both fall over the edge, and I fill this perfect pink cunt with my release as she finds her own.

I lower Pocket back to her feet and slide out of her. She whimpers at the loss of my fullness. I keep my hand on her hip. Echo glances up at me and slides between us, turning back toward Pocket. She drops to her knees and swipes her tongue up the length of Pocket's mound, slurping up my release that has escaped her channel. Pocket's whimper at the touch makes my dick twitch, readying itself for round two.

"I love you, both of you." Pocket's voice is just barely a whisper, but I hear it in the deepest parts of my soul.

I've been hunched over my computer for days looking for anyone who could be associated with the organization that had Echo. Part of me feels guilty because there is no guarantee that Ivy was with them, but what are the chances that we find Echo in a situation so like Ivy's? After everything I've witnessed during my search, my pussy tells me—because spidey senses have nothing on my pussy—that we're in the right hemisphere.

I scroll through the most recent information I was able to siphon from the CIA and FBI databases. They really should be better about their security protocols. It was child's play, really. You'd think that having two ghosts accessing files would sound alarm bells, but nope. They didn't notice that Supervisory Special Agent Daniels or Targeting Analyst Jameson were accessing secured servers when they've both been worm food for over ten years. Makes me question our national security, but I digress.

"What are you expecting to find?" Echo asks as she curls into AK's side while they watch some reality show on Netflix. I don't understand what the point of the show is; they're hiding from each other in a box and talking about themselves before they meet. Honestly, I stopped paying attention as soon as I realized AK was watching just to humor her. This is absolutely not my thing.

"A face that I'm hoping you recognize, so we can hunt them down and end them," I respond, the last half in song.

"You really need to stop watching the musical episode of Buffy to fall asleep." AK huffs out a laugh.

I shoot a glaring glance over my shoulder at him. Even if I'm giggling to myself, he's not wrong.

I pull up a file on someone flagged for potential association with virginal trafficking. Going over it line by line, I realize his last known location was local. Where we found Echo. I open the attached image of the guy James. It says he's six-feet-three-inches tall. The picture shows a man in his mid-thirties with dark hair styled similarly to Justin Timberlake's ramen, 'It's gonna be MAY' look.

Gross.

The deeper I search, the more it looks like he may be who I've been hunting. Multiple solicitation charges, corruption of a minor. I begin to shake the more I read. The anger that flows through my veins isn't uncommon, but this feels more personal. Echo will be with us, and if he is one of the men who hurt her... I take a deep breath and nod at AK who's been stealthily paying attention to me while they watch the show.

I lock my computer and put it on the table before walking away while they finish the episode. I don't have the heart to interrupt the joy written across her face when I know I'm about to tear her world apart. Again.

After twenty-three minutes and thirty-seven-and-a-half seconds, the episode is finally over. AK picks up the remote from the arm of the couch he's leaning against and stops it before the next one from starts.

Of all times to NOT ask if we're still watching. Thanks, Netflix.

Echo turns to AK and then back to me, a confused expression on her face.

"What's going on?" Her voice wavers with apprehension.

"Little Spark, I may have found one of the men," I pause, allowing my words to process. "Can you take a look and tell me?"

She stiffens in AK's arms. To his credit, he doesn't move, even though I can see it's killing him not to comfort her the way he wants, the way he does with me. She's been getting better, but in this moment, she's just not ready to be comforted by a man.

She looks at me, squaring her shoulders. "Show me." Her tone is full of a faux confidence.

I'm proud of her for putting on a brave face, but I worry it just may break her more if he turns out to be who I think he is. I move the cursor to wake the screen, typing in my password and confirming it's me through my phone. The screen illuminates with a picture of James Christan. I slowly angle the screen in her direction. The gasp that leaves Echo's lips is followed closely by the fiery need of vengeance I recognize in her eyes.

"That's him. That's James. He's the one who fucking cut me, who left me like this." She grabs her pussy.

Usually, I'd whimper at such a bold move, but right now, only one thought crosses my mind: I want to see everyone important to him go up in flames.

"The last time he was there, he told us that he would burn us before he took what he wanted from us." The venom she's spewing is overwhelming me, which should say a lot.

I nod and take the computer back to my lap.

"Give me until tomorrow. I'll find where he is, and we'll take care of it." I lean over and press a soft kiss to her forehead. "Knife Daddy, can you get supplies?"

AK cocks a brow at me, a silent conversation passing between the two of us.

*What supplies?* The confusion is written across his face.

*Ask how she wants to do it. This is for her, not us.* I roll my eyes at him.

*You really think she's going to want to be alone with me right now?* His eyes narrow on me.

"Guys, you know I'm right here, right?" Echo's voice cuts through the silence.

"Sorry, Sunshine." AK chuckles darkly. "How do you feel about going out with me for a bit?"

"I want him to burn." Her statement is so straightforward and unexpected.

AK and I look at each other, then back at Echo.

"He wanted to burn me, and I want to be there to see the skin melt from his body." Her expression is dark, and I love her for it. "To hear *his* screams this time."

"Jesus Christ, that's hot as fuck." AK smirks as he pulls her into a tight embrace, pressing his mouth to her hair.

"I guess 'Little Spark' is even more appropriate." I wink at her before I wave the two of them off to find what we'll need for our outing.

The moment I saw his fucking face, it was as though a switch flipped in my brain. Suddenly, all I could think was how I wanted to make him feel what he made us feel, only worse, so much worse. The pain and agony he made us feel every time he came to see us. The horrific things he did to our bodies, our souls.

*"I love the way it feels when you bleed all over me, just for me. The way my come mixes with your blood."* His lips pressed against the column of my throat as he spoke, thrusting inside me like I was his fuck doll. *"The way you scream when I slice your skin apart makes me so fucking hard, dollface."*

"Sunshine, where did you go?" AK's voice pulls me from the dark memories.

"Nowhere important." I lean into him as we close the distance between the entrance to Pocket's apartment and the van they brought me here in almost two months ago.

AK opens the passenger side door for me, pressing a gentle yet firm hand against the small of my back. The warmth from his palm against my skin fuels my desire for vengeance, giving me the strength to continue with what I plan.

I pry my eyes open as I wake, my body feeling too warm. Turning my head, I realize I'm wrapped in AK's arms, the heat from his body like a furnace. His deliciously sinful scent of whiskey and sex have me feeling things I never felt for a man. Reaching out for Pocket, my hand meets the cool sheets on her side of the bed, telling me she's been gone a while. I attempt to untangle from the giant man behind me, but as soon as I try to slide out from under him, he pulls me in tighter.

"Where are you going, Sunshine?" he grumbles into my ear, burying his face in the crook of my neck. It sends chills down my spine that settle in my core.

"She's not in bed. She needs sleep. Plus, you smell like her, and it's making me feel things," I groan.

"Oh? I'm making you feel things, Sunshine? I can make you feel even more whenever you want." His velvety chuckles instantly have my pussy convulsing with a need that only my Angel can satiate.

He reluctantly releases me. I roll to the side of the bed, sitting up and placing my feet on the floor, stretching my back before I stand. I turn back to see AK's eyes locked on me as I walk toward the living room. With a soft giggle, I shake my head and set out to find my woman.

As soon as I enter the living room, I see her at her laptop, a cup of steaming coffee next to her. Her vibrant blue hair is wrapped in a tight bun at the base of her neck. She doesn't even notice me approaching until I climb onto the couch behind her, wrapping my arms around her waist.

Pocket jumps from the couch, spinning around in the blink of an eye, and pins me to the couch. I squeal at the sudden movement.

She instantly relaxes when she sees it's just me, shifting into the gentleness I've grown accustomed to with her. "Fuck, Ech, you scared the shit out of me. Are you ok?"

"I'm ok. I didn't mean to startle you." I smile sweetly up at her. "I woke up and you weren't in bed. He smells like you and, well, it made me want you. Need you."

A devilish grin lifts her lips. I wrap my arms around her neck, pulling her down to me, her luscious chest pressing against mine. The feel of her pebbled peaks against my sensitive skin has me writhing beneath her. I bring my lips up to meet hers, getting lost in a kiss so deep and sinful it's likely illegal in most states. After several moments she pulls away, her icy-blue eyes trained on me.

"Oh, Little Spark." She presses her warm center against my thigh, and I buck up against her needing friction.

"Please, Angel?" I whimper.

"I want you. I always want you, sweet girl." She tries to smooth the coming rejection. "But I can't step away from this tonight, Ech. I'll make it up to you tomorrow, as soon as we're home, ok?"

I whine again and thrust up against her thigh once more, knowing she can feel my arousal. She doesn't speak, only stands up and holds her hand out to me to help me to my feet.

"Go get some sleep. I'll be in when I'm done. We'll leave as soon as I know everything I possibly can." Gently lifting my hand to her lips, she presses a sweet, soft kiss against my palm before continuing. "We need to make sure we have everything before we make a move if we want to get out of there alive."

I feel a frustration building between my thighs the farther I walk from her. Instead of lying in bed, I make a beeline for the bathroom. A groan builds in my throat, but I swallow it. I know she's busy, and I can't be mad at that, especially when what she's busy doing is for me. I need to relieve the pressure though. I can't wait. I twist the handle to turn on the shower, and I quickly undress while it heats up.

Stepping inside, I enjoy the warm, rhythmic pressure shooting down from above, letting it work through the muscles in my shoulders when I turn toward the spray. A sly smirk tugs at my lips as I lift my hands to reach for the shower head, ready to find my solace. I smile to myself when I finally get it down and point the running water toward my body, lowering it to my core.

The staccato beat from the heated stream has me tilting my head back against the wall of the shower. Feeling myself climbing higher up the cliff that leads to the most delicious kind of ecstasy. I lift my head, raising my eyes when I hear a creak through the sound of the water. My gaze meets a steel gray stare through the steam of the shower in the reflection of the mirror. I gasp, jerking my free hand to my chest, wrapping it around my throat. When I realize it's AK, I smirk at him. Knowing he's watching me makes this even hotter. I may not be ready for him to touch me yet, but I enjoy knowing his eyes are on me when I reach the point of no return.

My eyes remain locked on his as my resolve to remain quiet fails. Now that he knows what I'm doing, I can't keep myself under control. I snake my hand from my throat down to my breasts, squeezing each one gently, teasing my nipples, so he can see their immediate response. Gliding down my stomach to my hips, my fingers trail along the skin just above my pussy. Tapping softly at the sensitive flesh above my clit, I buck my hips in an attempt to get closer to the pressure the shower head is providing.

I whimper a little louder as I lower my hand, using my fingers to spread myself open, allowing easier access. I've barely opened myself up when the world around me is overtaken by darkness. I detonate when the powerful stream hits the right spot on my sensitive nub one last time. I scream out at the feeling, this time, though, it's his name on my lips as I shatter.

Soft whimpers pull me out of my restful state. I notice a light on in the living room, and I peer through the doorway, seeing Pocket still hard at work on her computer. I notice Echo isn't with her, and my heart thumps in my chest as anxiety builds. I've become so attached to this girl; the thought of her being upset pisses me off. I notice a light peeking through the bathroom door. Coming from behind it, are the same sounds that woke me. I stride toward the noise, closing the distance between me and whatever may be waiting for me on the other side of that door.

I press my hand to the wood doorframe, catching sight of Echo. She's leaning against the wall, her back arched and her head resting on the tile. Her body is so soft and smooth in all the right places. The shower head is hovering over her pussy, the water pulsing at her core.

Ahh, that explains the whimpers.

I smirk as I watch her. Echo's gaze meets mine, and with a gasp, she covers her chest with her free arm, grasping her throat. It doesn't take long before she finds her release once she sees me. My cock is hard as stone when I watch her come undone, my name on her lips.

"Sunshine, why didn't you just ask for help? You don't need to take care of yourself." A smile pulls at my lips when she turns the water off and opens the shower door. Holding a towel open as she steps out, I wrap her in the soft fabric, then my arms.

For the first time, she allows me to hold her like this. She's come so far. Yea, we may cuddle in bed but not like this, not after she just got herself off.

"AK," she whispers as she raises her chin, an intense look in her eyes.

"Hmm?"

"I don't know if I'm ready for more, but will you kiss me?" Her voice is so soft; I nearly miss it.

I grip her hips, pushing her back until her body is flush against the wall. I drag my hands slowly up the contours of her body until one hand is caressing her cheek, and the other hand cups the back of her head. Tilting her face up, I lean down, closing the distance. Internally scolding myself for being so eager to taste her firsthand. Her breath catches in her throat just before I make contact. I press my lips against hers, and she lets out a soft moan, opening just enough for me to get a taste. And holy shit, what a fucking taste it is.

Her sweet vanilla flavor explodes on my tongue, pulling a groan from deep in my chest. I move slowly in a nearly impossible attempt to keep myself from pushing her too far too fast. She whimpers and lifts her hands to my hair, digging her nails into my scalp as she holds me close. The way this woman's tongue is working against mine has my already hard cock straining against the waistband of my gray sweatpants, weeping and ready for whatever she'll give me. I pull away, panting heavily, brushing a stray strand of hair from her face.

For the first time since we met, she's holding my gaze, allowing me to really see her. The sparkle in those jade orbs melts the coldest parts of my dark heart.

"Sunshine, that was…" I shake my head, dragging myself away from her. "Fuck."

"What?" Her eyes go round in fear, an anxious crease marring the smooth skin of her forehead. "Did I do something wrong?!" The alarm in her question has me closing the distance between us again, pressing my length against her belly, eliciting the most delectable gasp from the petite little firecracker in front of me.

"The only thing you did was make it even harder to be a gentleman where you are concerned." I groan at the delicious bit of friction her body provides when she shifts on her feet. Even that small bit of connection has me wishing I could sink into her.

"Oh"—her face heats at my admission—"I'm sor—" she starts.

"Absolutely fucking not. You do not apologize to me. Not for that, not ever." I cut her off with a growl. My tone is gruff, and she looks startled at my seriousness. "Sunshine"—I move to cup her jaw, tiling her face so she's staring into my soul as I speak—"I will not push you. I respect you, your decisions, and your body. Do I want to get a taste for myself? Fuck yes, I do. Do I want to feel you wrapped around my cock, quivering with a release you should have been granted every time anyone has ever dared enter you? Fucking right, I do. The difference between what you experienced before and what you have with us: I will not take you without your consent."

Her eyes are glassy with unshed tears as I continue. I smirk at her, caressing her cheek with my thumb.

"It's only a matter of time before you realize the inevitable, just like Pocket did." My lips turn up into a grin as I lean down, pressing my cheek against hers, whispering into her ear, "You're mine in all the ways you deserve to be, and I will treat you like the queen that you are."

"AK." My name is a whisper on her lips. "I— Thank you." Silence fills the space around us as she presses her forehead to my chest. I hold her like a prized possession, my arms banding her against me. Pressing a soft kiss to the top of her head, I inhale her sweet scent. It's new, intoxicating, and different from the citrus fragrance of Pocket's shampoo. Some green bottle with what looks like an avocado on it. It doesn't make sense to me either. Echo, though, there is something so sweet, like an aroma of vanilla and honey. Between the two of them, it feels like I've finally found my way home.

"Will you lay with me?" Echo breaks the silence lifting her chin, the way her eyes light up when she looks at me now stealing my breath.

"Always, Sunshine." I study her face for another long moment, lost in her beauty. "You're fucking stunning." She giggles nervously, shaking her head as she turns back toward the bedroom. She's still wrapped in the towel, so when she climbs onto the king-size mattress, parts of her tight body peek out. She's filled out some since being here with us, and my heart swells at the knowledge she's letting us take care of her. The towel falls away as she sits at the head of the bed, her peachy nipples erect and begging for attention. Spreading her legs, she exposes her bare pussy and the scars that crisscross her skin. But seeing them only has my blood running hot with desire. A deep sense of pride fills my chest, that she is so confident to show me these parts of herself even after everything she's endured and the pieces she tries to hide from Pocket.

"Fuck. Me." I groan as I cross the room in a few long strides. "You're killing me, Sunshine."

"I need this," she whispers. "Please?" The plea is such a stark contrast to the confidence she just displayed.

"I want to, Sunshine, I really fucking do, but my hands wander when I sleep. I'm not going to take that chance until you're ready." I sigh as I pull my shirt over my head to hand to her.

"I won't know if I'm ready until it happens." She holds my gaze. "I need this." She repeats the words, no longer a question but a demand.

I've never felt this comfortable with a man before. Not even in my old life, not ever. AK has this way of building my self-confidence, letting me know I am always in control of what happens. I pull the covers over me, turning my back to him in the hope he'll wrap himself around me.

"Sunshine, I don't know about this." I feel the bed dip as he sits down.

"I trust you, completely. You won't hurt me." I reach back for his arm and pull him down so that he's spooning me.

"Do you want a blade, just in case?" he whispers into my hair.

A giggle erupts from my chest, and I can't help but pull him in closer.

"Shut up." I pause. "What does AK stand for? Knife Daddy just doesn't feel right coming from me."

"Ahh, Sunshine. Even Pocket doesn't know that. Maybe one day. Call me whatever you want. I'm not going anywhere." I feel him bury his face into my shoulder, the scruff of his stubble tickling my neck as he nips the sensitive skin. A soft moan passes through my parted lips, and I push my ass back against him. His fingers dig into my hips, holding me still. "Go to sleep, beautiful."

After a few moments I feel his breathing even out, his chest rising and falling so rhythmically it lulls me into a dreamless sleep for the first time in years, my body finally safe with him by my side.

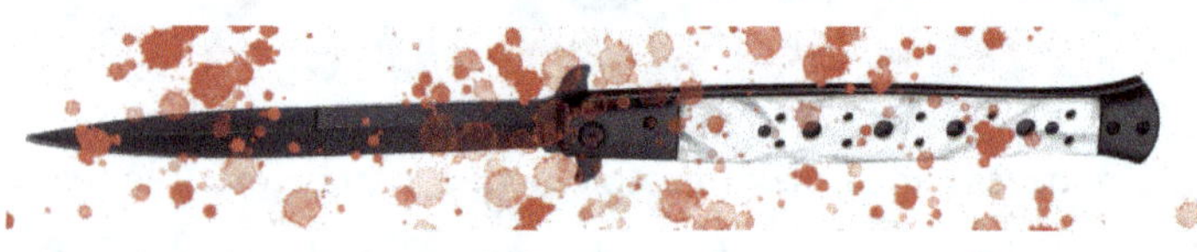

Thick, muscular arms are holding me tightly in place, one snaking between my breasts, so his hand is at my throat. He's barely applying any pressure, which makes no sense. They never care about that—the pain or discomfort—just about my compliance. The more I would fight, the worse it was.

My eyes fly open, my heart stuttering in my chest, as I let out short breaths, taking in my surroundings. It's not until I feel AK's thick length and piercings grinding against my ass that I realize I'm at Pocket's and that I'm ok. I let out a soft gasp when his hand travels down my soft stomach until his fingers are brushing against my pussy.

My core heats under his touch, proof of the needy little bitch she's become since they brought me here pooling between my thighs. I whimper as AK teases me with feather light strokes. I grind my ass back against his stiff cock through the sweatpants he insisted on wearing. Soft moans escape my lips when he dips his fingers between my folds, exploring the area of my body I am most ashamed of after what happened to me. But right now, under his touch, I can't seem to care about anything but what he's doing to me. For someone who murders people for a living, he's so gentle with me.

"Bear, please," I groan as I buck my hips into his hand. Suddenly his hands freeze. I can tell the moment he is fully conscious before he speaks. "Please, Bear," I beg again.

"Who the fuck is Bear?" His possessive growl only adds to my arousal.

"You," I whisper as he raises himself up to his elbow, looming over me with his eyes fixed on mine. "You're a teddy bear for me and Pocket, but a grizzly bear with everyone else." I feel my cheeks heat under his gaze.

"I don't know how I feel about that," he declares, leaning down, pressing his forehead to mine.

"Can you figure it out later? You woke me from a very peaceful sleep, and I enjoyed where it was going, Bear." I smirk with my new-found confidence. The exhilarating and maddening emotions I feel under his gaze, his touch. I'm already so needy; I can't imagine ever having this with another man.

The smile that pulls at his lips is the same one he directed at me when I first got here. If I weren't already a goner, that right there would have sent me over the edge. His mouth crashes against mine, our tongues clashing together in an all-out war of exploration. I moan into him as his fingers dip between my folds once more, his thumb caressing the swollen, sensitive bundle of nerves. He pulls away from our kiss to lock eyes with me as he plunges his fingers inside me.

"Fuck, Bear! Yes!" I cry out, filled with a growing need. I buck my hips up to meet his long, thick digits, needing more of him.

"Sunshine," he croons as he dips his head and presses a soft kiss against my shoulder. "I need to taste you."

It's not a question, it's a fact. One that even if he were asking and not telling me as a way to prepare myself for what he has planned, I wouldn't be able to say no. I need this as much as he does. I may need it more, to fully heal. I need him to claim me the way Pocket has. With a gentle nod of my head, I whisper, "Yes."

He begins pressing soft kisses down my body. His stubble scratches against my already heated skin. The man knows exactly what he's doing, too. I'm all but begging for him to fuck me with his tongue when he finally slides it up my length, licking my arousal, cleaning me like I'm the spatula he used to mix a cake batter. Making sure to get every last drop.

My legs are shaking by the time he lifts my knees over his shoulders and pulls my clit into his mouth with a suction force that I've never experienced and need to experience every day for the rest of my life. I scream as I detonate, begging him not to stop.

My eyes are closed tight as the orgasm rolls on for several long moments. I hear the commotion before I see her. Pocket comes in with a blade in her hand, ready to sink into the nearest flesh.

"Bear, fuck, yes. Oh my god! Don't stop," I sob as I writhe against him, needing more now that I've seen our girl. Because that's exactly what she is. Ours.

My mind is whirling with information when an alert chimes on my computer. A security camera caught James entering a roadside motel an hour away. I internally squeal, hoping not to wake them, but that's when I hear it. Whimpers with which I've become intimately acquainted. There's no way; I shake the thought from my mind. It's when I hear her scream that I can't stay still any longer. Jumping up from my spot on the couch, I snatch my blade from the table next to me before I close the distance between me and my bedroom.

I crash into the door, nearly tearing it from the hinges to get to her. It's then that I see Echo sprawled across my bed with AK face down between her thighs, her legs hooked over his shoulders. She looks so beautiful, the pure bliss on her face. Echo's eyes are closed so tightly, I can tell she's trying to hold onto the experience, willing it to last longer. She must realize I've come into the room because her eyes go wide, she takes me in, and that's when I see it. Another orgasm takes hold, her body shaking with release. The entire time her eyes are locked on me, the most beautiful sight I've ever witnessed.

"Fuck. Me," I whisper into the room.

Echo is still panting, trying to catch her breath, when AK chuckles darkly from between her thighs. He swipes his tongue up her length again, and I can see the arousal coating his tongue before it disappears into his mouth. He stands, a wicked grin plastered across his beautiful face. In one quick stride, he reaches me, gripping my chin between his fingers and pressing his lips against mine. I gasp at the scent of her on him, moaning into him, my lips parting to allow him entry. It's then that a sweet tangy flavor explodes on my tongue as he passes the last of his feast into my mouth.

Somehow, I find the strength to pull away. My eyes dart back and forth between the two of them, and I feel my lips twist into a genuine smile as the possibilities of what this could mean for us race through my mind. I can't think about that now, though. I clear my throat.

"When I tell you we will continue when we get back, I mean I am going to feast on your cunt as you ride his cock of steel, all while he is restrained." I press a quick kiss against AK's lips before lowering myself onto the bed Echo is still sprawled out on. A serene expression still on her face as I gently nip her jaw, grazing my teeth along the sensitive skin. "I want to witness you choking on his cock with that pretty little pussy." The gasps coming from Echo have me ready to say fuck it, but I know this needs to be done before we can get lost in each other.

"What did you find?" AK asks, sensing where my mind is.

"I know where he is. He's about an hour away, so if we leave now"—I glance at the time, seeing it's after ten in the morning—"we can be done by night fall."

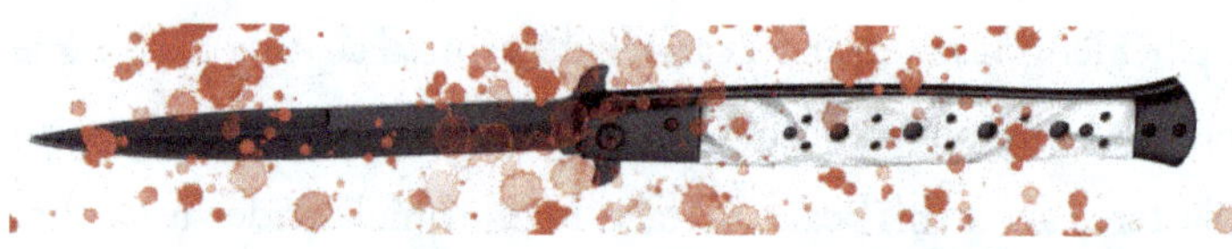

As soon as they come out of their post-orgasm haze, we are able to get on the road fairly quickly. The van smells like sex, and AK has been pitching a tent since we left, but I can't be mad at that. We finally pull up to the motel after a little over an hour drive. Paying attention to traffic laws is no fun at all, but I also don't want to deal with the police. While I'm not against killing law enforcement—since there are so many corrupt motherfuckers hiding behind the badge—I have a one-track mind right now. *Helping my woman fulfill her need for vengeance comes first.*

I've had an eye on the security feed since I saw the fucker go inside, so I know he's still here. Before pulling up, I quickly place the feed on a loop to avoid any unwanted eyes catching us. AK parks up close to the door I saw James enter earlier. I tuck my hair inside one of my muted wigs so as to not stand out before I exit the van and stalk around the building, checking for any other exits we need to be concerned about. Relieved to find that there is nothing more than an air conditioner unit for each of the rooms hanging out of what looks like it could have once been a window, I make my way back to the others. With a slight nod toward the van, I see AK's chin dip in response. Taking a deep breath, I close the distance between myself and the door that James is hiding behind. I knock lightly and put my mask of innocence in place.

I hear rustling and grumbles behind the door a few seconds before it cracks open, a tall man appearing through the small opening. Batting my lashes at him in an attempt to flirt, I smile shyly before speaking.

"Hi there, sir." I purr the last word of my greeting, knowing it will keep his attention on me. "My car broke down, and I was wondering if you'd let me use your phone."

"Well, I can't let a little lady like yourself be stranded on her own." An audible creak sounds as he opens the door wider, allowing me to see him fully. He's shorter than AK, maybe five-foot-ten with a beer gut and disheveled dark locks that show off the worst receding hairline. I smirk as he steps aside with a twisted grin on his face, allowing me entry.

"Thank you so much, sir." Giggling, I allow the display of naivete work on my behalf.

Once I'm inside, I glance around the space confirming my suspicion that he was alone. Before I have a chance to continue the ruse of using the phone, he's on me. A thrill runs through me as I lean into his hold which throws him off guard long enough that he doesn't realize I have my blade in my hand. I spin around to face him while he's taken aback, holding the knife to his throat.

"Oh, sir," I purr again, "You didn't think it would be that easy to get a *little lady* like me in your room so easily, did you?"

I bring my knee up to his groin with a quickness he doesn't see coming. The impact has him on his knees a second before AK and Echo are in the room with us. A wicked grin full of pride stretches across my Knife Daddy's beautiful features while an expression of worry is etched across my Little Spark's face.

"Are you ok?" Echo asks as she hovers behind AK's formidable presence.

The ride to the abandoned barn Pocket found while looking for him—and a place to play out my deepest vengeful desires—is only supposed to take an hour. We move slowly through the streets to ensure no one is following us. I'm sitting in the passenger seat, my knees pulled into my chest, my arms wrapped around my legs and face buried into myself. I can feel his gaze on me. Heat prickles through me every time his eyes land on me since we finally crossed the line this morning. He doesn't speak, though I feel the heat of his palm against my thigh, offering a silent comfort I didn't think would be possible from a man.

James is in the back of the van, tied up with Pocket watching him. I can't bring myself to look back to check on her. I know she's ok though. She took him down so easily back in that motel room. She can handle herself. She's prepared, unlike me.

When I saw his face, even contorted in pain, I was taken back to the time he had me chained up and taking a razor to my pussy. Seeing Pocket standing over him was overwhelming. He and

Chris are the reason my best friend is gone. He is the reason that I am deformed. I will make him pay. Not only for me, but for her, too.□

I barely register the motor turning off and no longer being in motion when AK clears his throat. "Sunshine, are you sure—"□

"Don't finish that question or that line of thought. I may be in my head, and I may have never taken a life before, but I have been dreaming about ending this motherfucker for years." I pause. "He didn't just hurt me, James and Chris. They both—" The words die on my lips as I lift my head, raising my eyes to meet his. I don't continue. I can't, but I know that he understands. He knows why I haven't gone into detail.□"You can't take this from me."□

With a gentle nod and a soft, encouraging smile, AK lets himself out of the driver side door. Taking a deep steadying breath, I follow close on his heels, meeting him at the back of the van. He and Pocket struggle with getting James out of the back. It's not until she elbows him in the temple that his body goes slack, allowing the two of them to execute the plan and get them into the barn.

I close the doors to the van before following behind, dragging the metal chair behind me. The loud scraping sound against the gravel sends chills through my body. When I finally get it in place, we work together, stripping James down to nothing and getting him confined to the chair—this time with actual chains. For what I have in mind, AK says that the traditional zip ties won't work. □

When we're sure he's not going anywhere, I step back, admiring my handiwork of his arms chained separately to the back of the chair when a set of strong arms wrap around my torso. Holding me tight against a warm chiseled chest I've become all too familiar with, I find comfort here even in the chaos. I cover his arms with mine, holding him to me. Pocket steps in front of us and smiles up at AK before her eyes meet mine. I relax even more into AK at the sight of her before me.□□

"Little Spark, if you need out, you just say the word, and we'll take care of him. Ok?" She keeps her eyes locked on mine as she nods her head to James' back before us. I know she's looking for a reaction. Waiting for me to freak out but, quite honestly, I don't have it in me to freak out. I hate him, for everything he's done to me, to her, and for everything he stands for.□□

"I've got this, Angel." I smile at her, pulling her into the embrace. AK cages us both in his arms, not letting go for several minutes.□□

"Let's do this. I am strangely looking forward to getting home and letting y'all use me for your own pleasure, even if it means taking a syringe to the dick." He chuckles darkly at the agreement he and Pocket made a few days ago in the shower.□□

Pocket releases me, way too giddy for what we're about to do. I let out a giggle as she skips toward James. AK squeezes me against him while we watch the next few minutes unfold before us. Pocket doesn't speak the entire time. She circles James' body, still limp in the chair, like an eagle about to dive on her prey. She takes a predatory stance in front of him, cocking her head to the side looking down at him. In the blink of an eye, her hand crashes against his face, a loud crack echoing around the empty space.

"Ahhhhhhhh what the fuck?" James roars loudly.

"Oh, goody! You're awake!" The sing-song way the words escape her does things to me that should terrify me. In reality, I may be more attracted to this side of her than I should admit. "So, I just have a few questions for you and then we can get on with the fun stuff, ok? Lovely."

She is sure not to look behind him, to not give away that they have company. My skin is humming with anticipation. Ready to end him. To inflict even a fraction of the pain that he caused us. Pocket steps forward, straddling James' lap when AK stiffens behind me. It's quite adorable that he has no problem seeing us together, but Pocket with anyone else has him ready to be possessive as fuck.

I turn in his arms to face him, an innocent smile on my face as I press my palm to his cheek, directing his attention down to me. "Don't worry, Bear. She's still ours." The whispered acknowledgment has him relaxing into me. Turning back around to watch the show, I find I am just in time to see her blade against his jaw.

"I feel generous, considering I have no clue what's next for you. So I'll give you ten seconds to tell me where I can find Hymen." She stares down at him with a heated expression, unlike any I've seen before. She looks like she's about to eat him alive.

"I don't know. The last time I heard from him he was out of the country." The panic in James' voice sends excitement through my veins. "He—He said that he would be back in the area in a few weeks. If he doesn't intend to fuck the girls, or girl -now, he stays with his wife. They live on the south side in that gated community," he rushes out.

A fire burns through me at the mention of her. How he so casually forgot that he ended her life. I attempt to lunge for him, but AK has a tight hold on me as he whispers into my hair, "Not yet, Sunshine. Soon."

"Wild Acres? Is that the gated community?" Pocket arches a brow as she questions him. He nods his head vigorously in response. "Oh, goody! That wasn't so hard, was it?" She hops down off of his lap and steps back before subtly nodding to me. "So, now the fun part can begin! I believe you know my Little Spark."

AK presses a quick kiss to my hair again before releasing me. I close the distance between Pocket and myself, my arms crossed below my chest, which lifts my breasts to the gods. I smirk at James when understanding lights his face.

"Little Duck?" he whispers into the open space between us. "But how?"

"It's Echo, motherfucker," I snarl at him with a venom that makes Pocket gasp. I glance back at her with a wink that makes her giggle. Looking back toward James, I clear my throat before continuing. "Do you even remember all of the horrible things you've done to me? The scars you've caused? The pain I've endured at your hands?"

"I remember everything. You liked it! Don't act like you didn't!" He no longer sounds all big and bad like he used to.

"You think I enjoyed you disfiguring me? Both the internal and external pain? Oh, this is going to be more fun than I thought." The wicked laugh that passes my lips is a sound I've never heard come from me. To be fair though, I haven't had much to be joyful about over the past decade. Holding my hand out to Pocket, she knows what I'm asking for. Asking for it would just be a waste of breath. When the cool handle of the blade presses into my warm skin, a sigh of contentment passes through my lips. I take a few steps toward James, lifting the knife so that the light streaming through the windows gleams off the blade.

With a sly smile, I bring the blade down quickly, a brisk slice against his chest to start. I make a show of it, sure to cause enough pain but not so much damage that it takes away from my fun as I continue what I have planned.

"Did you think we enjoyed it when you cut into us and then forced yourself onto us?" I really don't care for a response. "That we wanted to feel our skin tear apart with every thrust into us?" I snap at him. I drag the blade down his chest, leaving a shallow gash in its wake. I get very enthusiastic with the knife in my hand being sure to leave cuts all up and down his torso. When he's cursing and whimpering so much it's no longer comical, I kneel before him.

"Let's see how much you enjoy it." I flash him a grin from between his thighs. Slowly and methodically, I carve a triangle around the base of his flaccid penis. Repeating the steps, making the triangle larger each time I cut into the skin.

"Please, stop. I'm sorry. I'm so sorry," he cries out, the pain overwhelming.

"Were you sorry when you and Chris forced *her* onto the hook and watched her be torn apart from the inside out?" I drive the blade into his thigh before standing. "I don't think you were. So, let's have some fun, shall we?"

Turning my back toward him, I glance at AK who smirks at me knowingly. He knows most of what I have planned. Without another word, he hands me a pair of rubber gloves, a sponge, and a small bowl of clear liquid. The scent of ethanol is so strong it's nauseating. AK follows me back over to James who looks like he's about to pass out.

"No, I don't think so." I slap his cheeks with my rubber gloves hard enough to bring him back to the land of the consciousness.

"Fuck off, you stupid cunt," he snarls at me, his head lulling to the side.

"Now, is that any way to talk to a lady?" AK growls at James, his fingers on his jaw, gripping him so tightly I can see AK's fingers turning white.

"I swear to fuck, Little Duck. I'm going to kill you when I get out of here," he snarls once more.

"Aw, it's cute that you think you'll be seeing freedom ever again, you psychopath." I smirk at him before calmly pressing my hand against AK's forearm. "Bear, it's ok. Just do what I asked."

No words pass between the two of us as I cover my hands in the rubber gloves and AK tapes James' mouth shut, cutting a hole just big enough for the flexible piping to feed through into his mouth. We hear some gagging noises as it's forced into the back of his throat which only makes it more exhilarating for me.

I dip the sponge into the gasoline and carefully tap along the cuts I made while my Bear pours a bit of gas into the tube lodged in James' throat. It's what I imagine a beer bong would look like just not as much fun. We used to watch movies and talk about what it would be like when we went to college. Obviously, that's never going to happen now. One day, I'm going to do a beer bong just for her, to check it off our list. I shake the thoughts of my best friend from my mind when James' screams become more unbearable.

Giggling, I step away long enough to grab the noisiest part of the plan. When I turn back to him, I hold up the string of firecrackers. "Let's see how much you have to say now."

It's easier said than done to shove the string of miniature explosives through the hole in the tape, and into this motherfucker's mouth. Once his mouth is filled enough that he can't speak, and the fuse is hanging from the tape, I step back, appreciating my handiwork.

AK stands next to me with two bundles of sparklers in hand. I'm quite giddy with excitement as I take them. Kneeling down, I take the sharp end of the sparkler and stab as hard as I can, breaking through the skin and muscle of the iliotibial band on the side of his leg, running from the hip to the knee. Part of the plan is to make the fear last as long or longer than the death itself. He deserves to suffer. With all the trauma we endured, there is no reason he should get out of it without the emotional turmoil along with the physical.

Once the second bundle of sparklers is embedded into his leg, I bring a lighter to the end of the stick, lighting it on fire and doing the same to the other. They both are so beautiful, and his screams are the icing on the cake.

"Are you going to light the fuse for his mouth?" Pocket asks, looking at me curiously.

"Not yet. That will happen on its own."

I look back at the scene before me, James bloody torso on display, and my heart is hammering in my chest. Though, after several long moments, I decide the sparklers just aren't working fast enough. With a knowing and wicked grin on my face, I pick up the can of gasoline that AK had set down on the ground. When I finally reach him, I lift the gas can as high as I can, pouring it all over him. Every inch of this piece of shit is now soaked in pure gasoline.

"If this goes like I expect it to, you're going to want to get as far away from him as you can," I call over to Pocket and AK, who are standing off to the side.

"Sunshine." AK's voice is strained.

"I'll be ok, I promise." I direct my smile at AK who is frowning. "We have plans tonight. Don't worry. I will be there." The man who has killed countless sick bastards in his life actually blushes at the reminder of what we have planned when this is done.

I shake my head, the smile never wavering. I gently pick up the fuse in my hand, stepping as far back as I can, knowing if I do this wrong, it will be all over for me. Carefully, I light the fuse, dropping it against James' chest as he screams unintelligibly through the tape. I rip it off as quickly as I can just before the telltale *whoosh* sounds, and he is engulfed by flames. It's such a beautiful sound. I'm shocked that I actually make it to the door just in time for the firecrackers to blow. Seeing what was once his head blow into pieces in the sky is so inspiring.

"God damn, Little Spark." I hear Pocket's voice before she wraps me in a hug.

We stand there for several moments watching as the fire burns high before we separate and gather supplies. Pocket is in the front seat next to me, ready to drive away when our man comes rushing out from the smoky barn and leaps into the back of the van, closing the doors behind him.

"Move it, Killer!" he calls over his shoulder at Pocket who steps on the gas. Turning onto the main road, I look in the side mirror and see the old building ablaze in orange flames in the distance. By the time anyone even realizes what's happened, it will be a pile of ash.

I can feel the adrenaline coursing through my veins the entire drive home. My body is vibrating with need. My legs are bouncing in place, trying to get out the extra energy from the high of what I just did. That was so thrilling—ending someone who was the most disgusting kind of evil.

"Little Spark, are you ok over there?" Pocket asks as she makes the turn off the highway back to our place.

"I'm just hyper. That was thrilling! Can we do it again?" I ask sheepishly. "Obviously not to good people but to more of those people."

AK chuckles darkly from behind us. "How about you let the high you're feeling wear off and then we can reassess your desire for getting bloody, Sunshine."

"Don't be a party pooper, Bear." I pout. "I have so much energy. I need to burn it off. I'm going crazy."

I glance out the window, realizing we're nearly to the apartment, and the organ in my chest starts thumping so hard at thoughts of what we're going to do. What I'm going to do. AK must notice the change in my mood because I feel him behind me.

"Sunshine, you don't need to do anything you don't want to." The whispered words hot on my skin as he leans in to make sure I hear him.

"No, I know that." I pause, turning in my seat to look at both of them. "I want to, just... slow?"

"You can go slow on him, but I want to taste you. The blood on your hands is too fucking sexy to waste," Pocket announces as she pulls the van to a stop, shifting into park. Before I can respond, she's got her seatbelt unbuckled, then climbs over the center console. Her legs land on either side of my thighs, straddling me. She wraps my hair in her fist, tugging gently to tilt my face to an angle that works for her. Once she can see my eyes, she dives in, her lips crashing against mine in a frenzy. Soft moans escape both of us as our hands roam along the other's body. It could be seconds or hours before a deep groan pulls us out of our haze of arousal.

"If you two don't get the fuck upstairs, I'm going to bend Pocket over back here and nail her ass while she goes down on you. While that sounds like fun, I want to feel your pussy strangle my cock, Sunshine."

"Fuck, that's hot." Pocket giggles before sucking my lip into her mouth and opening my car door to let herself out. "Let's go. With how hard he is already, I want to see if the injection makes him last longer or just causes pain."

"Why the fuck do I love your crazy ass?" AK chuckles darkly as he hops out the back of the van, closing the distance and slapping her ass playfully. Holding a hand out to me, he helps me to the ground.

"You motherfucker, that's the first time you say it?" Pocket turns on her heel and leaps into AK's arms.

They're both smiling like giddy teenagers finding love for the first time. It's precious. Shaking my head, I giggle and walk ahead of them, climbing the steps two at a time until I'm standing in front of our door. Entering the code, I let myself in and head to the bedroom. Stripping down to nothing, I walk into the attached bathroom and turn on the shower.

Standing there alone with my thoughts for a few moments as the water heats up, I smile to myself, proud of how far I've come in such a short time. I know I have so much more healing to do, but with these two by my side, I know I'll be ok. I step into the hot stream of water, allowing it to soak my hair and skin. I'm in the midst of lathering my hair with shampoo when AK and Pocket stroll in, stripping off their clothes too. They pile in the shower with me, all three of us taking turns under the hot rush of water. AK attempts to lean down to kiss me when Pocket grips his neck, her eyes locked on his. A possessive look darkening her icy-blue eyes.

"Nuh uh, not right now, Knife Daddy." She playfully slaps his face. "Right now, we get clean, and none of us get any play time until I have you tied up."

"Fuck." He growls which makes me giggle again. "Oh, you think it's funny, Sunshine?"

"A bit," I admit. "Whatcha gonna do about it, Bear?"

He quickly pulls me into him, pressing his thick length into my stomach, and that's when I feel something odd. I hadn't bothered looking at his dick before because I didn't expect to be interested in it, even all the times he and Pocket barely waited for me to leave the room, so they could have sex without me there.

"What is—" I gasp.

"Cock of Steel, or Superman if you're feeling feisty." Pocket giggles as we're finishing up. "Come now, I have plans for both of you."

Her devilish sass has me ready to follow any command she throws my way. Wrapping myself in a towel, I don't make it two steps before AK throws me over his shoulder and carries me to the bed, tossing me down.

"Oh my god," I squeal in excitement.

"Killer." He stands over me as he looks to the other side of the room where Pocket is standing with ropes in hand. "Exactly how long do you plan on having me restrained?"

"I don't know. I usually get off a handful of times before I'd end someone but since I want to keep you around. I'd say three each?" She sighs. "Why?"

"Because I'm going to play out that scenario I mentioned downstairs as soon as you two are done using me." He lowers himself, so he's looming over me, pressing a gentle kiss against my lips and trailing down to my jaw and neck.

"Bear," I whimper, "that's so not fair."

Pocket's wicked giggle from the other side of the room has my frustration at an all-time high.

"Don't worry, Little Spark. We'll take care of you." I look over just in time to see her wink. "Knife Daddy, get over here." She points to a dining chair she brought in from the other room, and with a snap of her fingers he obeys her.

I lift up to my elbows, watching as she wraps beautiful patterns onto his skin with the rope. I can't tear my eyes away, her own staring into his steely gray orbs. The care with which she restrains him makes my heart stutter and my core clench.

"Come watch, Little Spark." Her voice perks me up and draws me to her, and before I even realize it, I'm moving toward the two of them. "You ready?" Pocket's question is directed toward me, not AK. I nod my head, my eyes locked on his semi-hard dick. She kneels between his legs, holding onto his length as she pulls a syringe out of, I don't even know where. Putting the capped side in her mouth, she gently bites down and tugs, exposing the needle. She doesn't speak as she preps the injection and carefully yet quickly stabs AK's cock and pushes the cocktail through into his member.

A sharp intake of breath takes my gaze away from AK's already thickening cock, up to his face. A pained expression contorting his beautiful features.

"I'm fine, Sunshine. It just stung a little. You should have seen her when she would do this with someone she didn't like." He grins at me.

"Hey You," Pocket interrupts. "No talking, Knife Daddy. You're our toy, toys don't talk." Her glare should frighten me, but really it only sends a fresh wave of heat to my core.

Pocket closes the distance between us, wrapping my hair in her fist once again, her free hand cupping my jaw. I tangle my fingers in her beautiful sapphire locks as our mouths crash together. Our tongues lash out at each other, trying to get closer. I whimper softly as she glides her soft, silky fingers down my neck, then slowly trailing down my body. Stopping only briefly to tweak my nipples and then making her final descent to my pussy. As soon as her fingers graze my clit, I grind against her, looking for more friction. She smiles playfully, knowing exactly what she's doing.

"Little Spark," she whispers against my lips as she slowly pulls away. "I want you to straddle his legs. You can have his dick against your back. I just want to make you come while you're on him. Ok?"

"Ye—ye—yes," I whimper, the neediness in my voice surprising me.

I turn to face AK, needing to see his face once more before my back is to him. It was like this too often with the others. He offers a gentle smile before nodding at me, a simple acknowlededgment that nothing will happen that I don't want to. I lean in, pressing a soft kiss to his lips—a gesture of thanks—before turning my back to him. Climbing on top of him, it feels strange sitting like this. My legs are hanging on the outside of his thighs, straddling him, opening myself up fully to the room. To my Angel.

Pocket doesn't speak to me this time. She stalks over like a lioness about to pounce on her prey. As soon as she's standing in front of me, her hands lightly grip my thighs before she drops to her knees before me, staring up as if she's about to pray to the heavens. I gasp as soon as she strikes. Her mouth connecting to my pussy, tongue lashing out and swirling around my clit. I scream out, grinding my hips, trying to increase the friction.

"Oh, god. Please, Pocket!" I scream, gripping her beautiful blue mane between my fingers. I hear a strangled groan from behind me, realizing that I'm torturing AK as much as she's torturing me. It gives me pause, realizing I have as much power as she does. "I need more!" I cry out to Pocket, gyrating my hips, still trying to get more friction from her but also teasing my Bear.

With a wicked smile, Pocket presses a soft kiss against my thigh and then looks up at me. "You only get my tongue. If you want more, you know how to get it." With a wink, she disappears between my thighs again.

"Jesus, fuck," I groan, throwing my head back against AK's shoulder. Lost in a near climax before she pulls away again, my head lulls to the side, exposing my neck to him. He angles himself to nibble on my neck, enjoying the frustration Pocket's causing me almost as much as she is from his reaction. I contort my arm behind my back, gripping his cock of steel. He lets out a sharp gasp when he feels my hand around him, and he bites into my skin, sending a jolt of excitement to my core. I nearly burst at the seams at the intensity of the moment, when I know that's not what our girl is aiming for.

"I need more, let me." The soft pleas are nearly inaudible, yet I know AK hears me because he groans into my neck again. With one last swipe of her tongue along my folds, she sits back on her heels, watching me, waiting for my next move.

I take a deep steadying breath before I lift myself as best I can. Maneuvering my hand between my legs to pull AK's cock from behind me. I line him up with my entrance, my eyes on Pocket, who has an excitement on her face that I haven't seen before. Fuck, she's gorgeous. I slowly lower myself onto him. His blunt head barely notching inside my entrance, and I'm panting.

"Jesus fucking Christ, Sunshine," AK grounds out behind me. "You are so god damn fucking perfect."

I whimper, unsure if I can take anymore. He's so big, and the piercings feel so strange. But god, I need more. It feels too good. Pocket is suddenly in my face, her lips ghosting over mine, letting me know she's there. I stare into her icy-blue eyes as I continue lowering myself onto him inch by inch until he's fully seated inside me. I'm already panting with need.

"Good girl, Little Spark. You're doing so well." Her voice is so gentle, it's unlike her usually possessive attitude when we're in bed together. Though we're not in bed, are we? "Now, you don't need to do anything. Just enjoy the feel of him filling you."

I'm experiencing a sensation overload; her words aren't making any sense. I think I get out a "MmM" before she disappears again.

The overload continues even further when I feel her mouth on me again. Circling my hips with AK's cock buried so deep inside me while her tongue is lashing out again, finding the most sensitive places she can reach. Sucking and swirling until I can't hold back anymore. I cry out, my head falling back on AK's shoulder once more. I feel my pussy convulsing around him. Squeezing him so hard as I fall over the edge, my vision going dark when I finally reach the crescendo.

"Fuck, Angel, Bear!" I cry, "Fuck!"

I hear AK roar behind me as my pussy walls continue to clamp down while I ride out the orgasm for several moments.

"You did so good, Sunshine." AK is panting. "Killer, I love you, but if you don't untie me, so I can fuck you so hard into the bed you have bruises on your ass from my hips slamming into you, I'm going to turn your ass so red you won't be able to sit for a week when you do finally let me out."

I can tell Pocket is just as affected as I am because she doesn't fight me when I tell her to untie me. She helps Echo stand, removing her from my aching cock. She gets Echo situated on the bed before returning to me. I'm going to enjoy the moment she lets me take her like I want, fully using her for both of our enjoyment. She feels so good. The way she clamped down on me as she came has my cock throbbing at the memory. The excitement in Pocket's eyes as she goes to untie me mirrors my own.

It takes her less time to untie me than it did to tie me, thank fuck. As soon as I'm free, I stretch my limbs before standing. Once I'm on my feet, I'm moving. My hand wraps around my Killer's throat, backing her onto the bed where Echo is sprawled out and waiting for us. I press my lips against Pocket's, swiping my tongue against her. Tasting my Sunshine on her has a possessive growl rolling from my chest. Pulling back, I drag my eyes from her icy-blue orbs to Echo, who is still blissed out on the bed.

I release Pocket, one finger at a time and crawl up Echo's frame, pressing soft kisses against her lips and slowly trailing down her body. The scruff of my beard makes her gasp every time I move lower. When I finally reach the apex of her thighs, I inhale, taking in the intoxicating scent of her arousal. I swipe my tongue up the length of her pussy, swirling quick tight circles around her clit, which makes her already humming body buck at the sensation. I chuckle darkly, enjoying the taste of her before I stand back up and look to find Pocket staring at me in wonder.□□

I drag her back to me, kissing her again, this time forcing my tongue in her mouth so she can taste Echo on me. She moans loudly. Her hands are in my hair, gripping so tightly it hurts in the best way. I grip her ass, spreading her cheeks apart, and swipe my fingers along her folds. She's squirming against me, so needy for more. I pull away and turn her toward the bed, a quick smack on the ass before lifting her so her knees are on the bed. She kneels in front of me on all fours. Pocket's arms wrap around Echo's thighs and pull her so that she's right in front of Pocket's face. It's a beautiful fucking sight.□□

I take my place behind Pocket's ass and notch myself at her entrance. Giving no real time to prepare or adjust, I slam myself inside her to the hilt. She lets out a loud pleasure filled scream as she lowers her mouth to Echo's cunt, lapping up her arousal. The room is filled with sexual noises, grunts, groans, and moans.

I can tell the moment that my Killer inserts her fingers inside Echo's pussy. The gasp that escapes her nearly sends me over the edge. Slamming my hips against Pocket's ass with every thrust inside her tight channel has me nearing release. I lean down, wrapping my arm around Pocket's torso I find her clit, pinching it between my fingers, making her scream into Echo's cunt. She squeezes my cock so hard I feel pressure building at the base of my spine, needing to fill her, but the fucking injection won't allow that. It's almost painful. I continue thrusting inside her, a string of curses passing my lips as I feel a need building even more inside me.

Pocket whimpers as she comes down from yet another release. "Knife Daddy, I need a minute. Ech?" □

I stare down at Echo whose eyes are alight with excitement. She nods cautiously. The longing I've felt for this woman, to finally have a chance to fill her. I groan and flop onto my back on the bed. □

"Sunshine, I'm going to need you to take control. I don't want to hurt you." □□She doesn't speak. Just lifts herself to her knees and straddles me, slowly sinking onto me. "Fuck." □

A soft moan escapes her as she fills herself with my cock. My god, she feels so incredibly good. Echo starts rocking slowly back and forth, getting comfortable in a position she's not familiar with. When she finally starts lifting herself up and dropping back down, I fist the sheets underneath me, so I don't bruise her from my grip. □

Pocket shifts next to me, and I glance over to see a wicked smile on her face before she slides down the mattress. "Little Spark, I want you to keep moving but Daddy is going to bend his knees and thrust up into you a little bit. Ok?"

"MmM," is all that Echo is able to get out, so I take that as a yes and lift my legs, bending at the knee and thrusting up. We both groan at the sensation.

I feel Pocket between my legs as I continue to thrust, getting deeper into Echo's perfect cunt. When I feel her fingers trailing down my thighs, I shiver, knowing exactly what she's planning. One hand leaves my thigh for a second before I hear an audible pop. She uses one hand to part my ass, and with the finger she just wet in her mouth, slides inside the tight ring of muscle.

"Fuck, Killer," I groan. Unable to stop myself anymore, I grip Echo's hips. Her eyes fly open at the sudden touch before rolling back into her head as I hold onto her tightly, thrusting even harder while Pocket toys with my ass.

Lifting one hand from Echo's hip, I move my fingers to her clit, pressing hard against her as she continues riding my cock. My vision starts to blur when Pocket finds the spot inside me that will end this. As Pocket maneuvers herself to massage my prostate, I pinch Echo's clit, her pussy convulsing around me, the pressure in my balls becoming too much. I explode inside her with a loud roar.

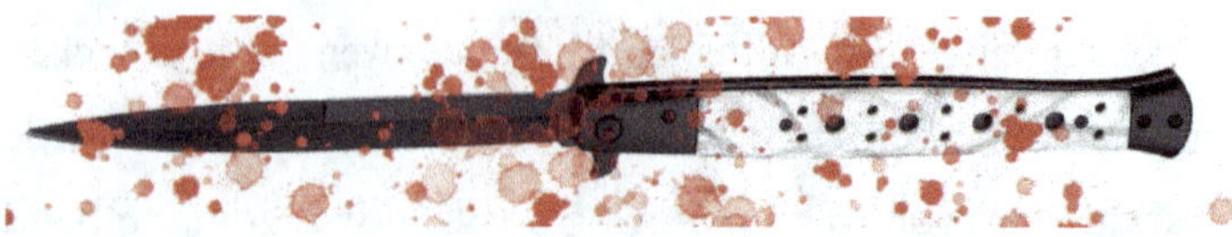

The following weeks are basically a montage of sexual experiences and exploration between the three of us. Getting to know one another's bodies in a way we hadn't before. Echo and I exploring each other and making up for lost time in a sense. Figuring how we all work together and separately.

"I want to take you two to dinner tonight," I announce as Pocket and Echo step out from the shower. "A real first date, for the three of us."

"I don't know," Pocket says as she blocks my Sunshine from view.

Does she realize how protective she is of Echo?

"Killer, it's dinner." I cock a brow at her. "I want to see how Echo reacts to something other than your damn cooking and takeout."

"It's ok, Angel. I want to go. I can't just hide away inside when we go off to take someone out." She laughs at her own joke. "I mean, I've never been on a date."

"You've..." The words die on Pocket's tongue, we both sometimes forget just how long she was held captive. "Go get ready." The response is clipped, and not up for further discussion.

I smirk, pulling Pocket into my arms. "I love you, Killer. Let's go give her a night to remember."

It takes them a few hours to get ready, between doing each other's hair and Echo putting on makeup for the first time since she's been here. Pocket puts on a light natural layer of makeup as well. I watch the two of them from my spot on the bed, just enjoying the view. So fucking beautiful.

I stand and close the distance between the three of us, walking into the bathroom and caging Echo against the vanity. She lets out a squeal and whips herself around to face me. A sinful smile on her face, I lift her onto the counter and part her legs. She's only wearing a bright pink thong and matching bralette. I dip my head and press my lips to hers, grinding against her center. She lets out a breathy moan. I hear Pocket panting from the other side of me. Pulling away from Echo, I turn to Pocket and go in for a kiss, but she surprises me, pressing her warm palm to my chest, pushing me away.

"Knife Daddy, we both know if this goes any further, we won't go out." Her sass is sexy as hell. "And it was your idea for this date. Get out, get dressed, and when we get home, you can fuck the shit out of both of us."

"Yes, please." My Sunshine endorses the idea.

Raising my hands in defeat, I back up, and Echo slides off the counter with a wicked smirk on her face. "Alright, I'll be a good boy and behave. For now."

Echo turns her back to me as she pulls on a white crop top. It's fucking gorgeous on her. The off-the-shoulder sleeves show off her collarbones and neck, making me want to nuzzle up on her and suck on the spot that always seems to make her beg for more. I hold off, though. Knowing what tonight means for her, I won't take that away. I want to show our girl an amazing night out. She deserves so much joy after all she's been through. Even if the dark skintight jeans she has on show off every curve, and I want to touch.

*Behave, Pocket.*

"God damn, Little Spark." I grin as her cheeks tinge pink at the compliment.

"Back at you, Angel." Her eyes shine with love. I know she hasn't said it, but I can feel it. With every look, every touch. She's just not ready to admit it to herself let alone to us.

It's wild to think that just a few months ago, I was completely on my own and now, I have these two partners that I couldn't live without even if I tried. They have become my everything. I'm not telling AK; he wouldn't let me live it down.

I put the final touches on my outfit, dressing up the black cut out mini dress with a pair of gold studs and a gold necklace AK bought me a few weeks ago. It's a near perfect mini replica of my favorite blade on a delicate chain. I open the bathroom door and see AK waiting for us in a pair of black slacks and a white button-down shirt. He looks like a god damn snack.

"Jesus fuck, Daddy." I'm all but drooling at the sight. "Momma likes."

"Damn, Bear." Echo is equally affected, considering how breathy her voice is.

"You both look— Fuck. Me." AK lets out a long whistle. "Stunning."

I smile up at him and twirl with a flourish. Echo is still standing in the doorway looking nervous as hell. I go to hold my hand out for her since she's usually still more willing to accept my encouragement. AK puts his hand up for me to stop. Arching a brow at him in question, I do, and he steps in front of me to speak to her.

"I have something for you." I hear him say in a low voice to her. "I'm going to step behind you, can you hold this for me?"

She blinks up at him, nodding, and taking a long, black, velvet box from him. I smile knowingly and stand back to watch their moment.

"Go ahead and open it, Sunshine," he says gently as he steps behind her, gingerly gathering her hair and placing it on one shoulder.

She opens it to display a necklace with a gorgeous pendant of the sun. She gasps, looking over her shoulder at him.

"Bear, this is—" she brings her hand to her chest, tears pricking at her eyes "—this is beautiful."

He lifts the necklace from the box to put in its rightful place around her neck. She spins around when he has it clasped, pressing a kiss to his lips and holding him tight against her.

"Thank you," she whispers as she pulls back before letting go.

"You're welcome, Sunshine. Let's go before you make it even more difficult to leave the apartment." He chuckles before taking both of our hands and leading us out the door.

I can't help but giggle when I see the table AK reserved for us. A round booth in the corner, partially hidden from the other patrons. AK sits between the two of us, a smile on his face as he wraps us in an embrace. We sit and chat for a while, AK and I share a bottle of merlot over the steak dinner. AK and Echo share a chuckle when I order a steak and lobster. Meanwhile, Echo lets out a delicious moan as soon as she tastes her chicken and asparagus over a wild rice pilaf that the server said pairs perfectly with a Pinot Noir. Apparently, they were right.

"Once we finish this, what do you have planned?" AK asks as I still next to him.

"Finish this as in, finding Ivy?" I stare at him with a hurt in my eyes that I know he can see.

"Yes, Killer. Once we finish this, you find her and get revenge on whomever it was that took her. What is your plan?" he asks as if it's not tearing me apart to have this conversation here.

"Bear," Echo whispers, quietly pushing him to change the subject.

"It's ok, Ech." I offer a weak smile before continuing, looking at AK. "I'm not sure what the plan is. I didn't expect to be in a relationship when I finished the plan, so I don't know."

"Fair enough." His deep chuckle makes me want to jump him, which just pisses me off even more. "I may have an option for you."

"And that is?" I hear the caution in my voice as we wait for his response.

AK doesn't get a chance to share his thoughts, though, when Echo freezes. Her breath hitches, and her face pales. I can't tell if she's breathing. She's staring out into the restaurant, not giving an inkling of what's happening.

"Echo, what's going on?" I reach over, pressing my hand on her thigh. Still with no response, I look up at AK who nods. I slide out of the booth and stand, allowing AK to slide her out with him and lift her into his arms. The sight of her looking so lost nearly breaks me.

It's not until we're back in the van, and I'm driving to the apartment while AK holds her in the back that she comes out of it. A loud shrill scream leaves her in a rush. I swerve at the sudden noise, nearly taking out a speed limit sign.

"Baby, it's ok. We're right here." I hear AK cooing in the back. "We're right here, baby. We're right here."

My heart aches that I'm driving and not able to be there for her right now, too, but I need to get us home.

"It's him. It's him. He's back," she sobs.

"What do you mean? Him who?" AK asks, not quite the brightest bulb right now, Knife Daddy.

"Ech, he's not supposed to be back for a few weeks," I pipe in from the driver seat, but as soon as the words leave my mouth, I realize just how fucking stupid we've all been.

*It has been a few weeks, we've been so wrapped up in one another, we lost track of time.*

It's him, it's him. How did he find me? How did he find us?

I have to tell her.

I have to break her heart all over again.

I feel AK's arms around me, holding me tightly to his hard chest as I internally spiral into my own thoughts. She'll never forgive me when she finds out. I'll lose her; I'll lose them both. Sobs rack through me as thoughts of what's to come flash through my mind. I don't know how long we've been back at the apartment when my surroundings come back into focus. I'm still in AK's arms with Pocket kneeling in front of me.

"Ech, talk to us." She tries to stay as calm as possible.

I look over my shoulder at AK, a knowing look in his eyes telling me it truly is time.

"The man who—"—I choke—"the man who had us—Johnny Hymen."

"Yea, what do you remember?" She stares into my soul with her penetrating eyes.

I sigh before continuing, "Your uncle Johnny. He's the one who had us."

"No," she gasps. "No, no, no!"

I can see the wheels turning and the moment she realizes what this means. I leap off of AK's lap and wrap myself around her, holding her as tight as I can.

"I'm so sorry, Angel. I didn't know how to tell you." Tears stream down my face as her body shakes in my arms. "I'm so sorry. I tried; I tried to keep her safe. I'm so sorry."

"No! They wouldn't. They couldn't!" She pushes me away and runs to the kitchen, barely making it to the trash bin before she retches, vomiting up everything she's eaten.

AK stands from his place on the couch and crosses the room in a few long strides, holding her hair off of her neck while her stomach expels its contents. He rubs small circles on her back in an attempt to soothe her. Considering the truth she's now faced with, I don't imagine it's going to help.

"Killer—" His voice is full of pain as he tries to speak.

"No, you knew. You knew who it was? You knew she was gone?" She spews the words, full of venom.

"I had my suspicions about Ivy. I didn't know who had them," he admits cautiously.

The room grows quiet, an uncomfortable silence that none of us seem ready to break. That is, until Pocket stands and goes into the bedroom. AK and I rush behind her to find she's digging through the closet. She pulls out an old box with Ivy's name on it. My stomach drops when she opens it and takes out things I haven't seen in years. Ivy's journal and her favorite stuffed animal from when we were kids. A Buffy figurine that she proudly displayed on her nightstand. I stumble as so many memories come rushing back.

She jumps up, wrapping herself around me, not allowing me to fall. AK is on my other side, helping me sit on the bed.

"I know." She lets out a strained sigh. "I know you didn't want to hurt me. You've been through so much. I understand why you didn't tell me."

She's always trying to protect me. It breaks my heart even more that I've brought on so much pain. "Angel," I choke.

"Hey, it's ok. We're ok," she repeats.

I sit staring off into space, not able to say anything else. Unsure of how much time passes before I find myself lying down on the bed. My heart hammers in my chest as thoughts of what's to come run rampant in my head. I don't register falling asleep until I hear whispered shouts from behind me. My eyes fly open to see Pocket and AK arguing in the living room. It's mostly Pocket yelling at AK who just sits there taking it.

"Please!" I call out, my voice shaking. "He didn't know. I never told him anything. I didn't want to risk losing what we were building." I sit back up, attempting to stand when they join me back in the room. "I know it was selfish, but I couldn't lose you two. Not after what I've already lost."

"Hey, Sunshine. It's ok." AK's velvety voice always blankets me in a sense of calm.

"You're not losing us, Little Spark," Pocket announces, "It's just going to take time to process."

"What can I do to help? How can I make it better?" I plead, needing to know she can forgive me.

I look between the two of them, hopeful that there is some way I can repair the damage I've caused. Pocket clears her throat and leans in, pressing a soft, chaste kiss against my lips. Doing the same to AK before standing.

"I want to watch you." Her smile doesn't quite reach her eyes. "The two of you, together," she clarifies.

"Killer, how is watching us fuck going to help you?" AK asks the question that I'm thinking.

"Don't question me. This is one of those times where you're going to be a good boy and do what I say." Her tone becomes domineering.

With a heavy sigh, AK turns to me. "She's going to instruct us. She's always held back with you. But right now, she's going to have me testing your limits. If at any point you want to stop or feel uncomfortable, let us know. Yea? Are you ok with that?"

My gaze darts back and forth between them. I hesitantly nod as I breathe out my answer. "Yes."

AK closes the distance between the two of us, my eyes locked on his gray stare. His lips crash against mine briefly until a throat clears, pulling us out the moment.

"Undress her." Pocket's instruction comes from the corner of the room where an armchair sits. I glance over to find her seated with her legs crossed like she's directing a show.

AK glides his fingers up my sides. It tickles as he does. When he reaches the hem of my white cropped shirt, he slides his fingers under and lifts it over my head. My bare breasts on display as he tosses the shirt off to the side. I try to lift onto my tiptoes to kiss him, but he drops to his knees before me. Unbuttoning and unzipping my jeans, he loops his fingers into the straps of my thong before he slides them over my hips and down my legs. I place a hand on his shoulder to steady myself as he helps me step out of them.

"Lay her out on the bed and make her come on your tongue." I barely register the words Pocket calls out as he stands, lifting me into his arms and tossing me onto the bed. "And don't fuck around. You and I both know you can get her off in a matter of seconds."

I squeak at the sudden movement. He chuckles darkly before his face disappears between my thighs, not giving me any time to prepare. The scruff of his beard no longer startles me the way it did before. I enjoy the vast contrast between Pocket's softness and his roughness. He wastes no time in getting me to the edge. My screams of pleasure fill the room as Pocket watches and instructs us on what's next.

"Good boy, you're both doing so well," I hear her praise from behind AK. "Now, I want you to fuck her. The way you fuck me. I want you to fill her with that thick cock of yours and make her beg you for more even when it hurts."

I gasp, fear enveloping me.

"Don't worry, Little Spark. It will hurt so fucking good you'll be pissed off when it's over." I hear the humor in her voice which allows me to calm.

AK crawls up my body, looming over me before he carefully notches himself at my entrance. I nod up at him, giving him an 'ok' to continue. As soon as he slides inside me, his piercings pressing so deliciously against my inner walls, I let out a whimper.

"That's right, Ech. He's going to use you so good."

Once AK is fully seated inside me, he groans, looking down at me with a question in his eyes.

"Yes, Bear. Fuck me," I beg.

It's all he needs before he's pounding inside me. Filling me repeatedly, so full my pussy is convulsing with a need for release. We're both groaning, the need mirroring in each of us.

"Don't you dare let her come yet. Pull out and flip her the fuck over. I want to see you take her from behind," Pocket orders from somewhere in the room.

The sounds of their pleasure travel through the apartment, becoming quieter the closer I get to the front door. I'm so careful to not make a sound as I unlock the deadbolts and turn the knob. I know they're lost in one another now, and I'm sure they'll be furious as hell at me when I get back, but my need to do this, to face my demon on my own, is too great. I can't wait for Echo to come to terms with the fact that she withheld information that should have been shared when we first found her.

I groan when I get to the parking lot, finding the van and AK's Suzuki Katana. Fuck, that bike is hot. I want Echo sprawled out on it while I feast on her pussy, and AK fucks me from behind. I shake the thoughts from my mind, knowing I can't go down that rabbit hole, at least not until I'm back. Crossing the distance to the van, I open the door and hop in. Even if it's going to be slower, there is no way in hell my Little Spark would get on the back of that bike.

I turn the key in the ignition; the engine roars to life, and I take off before they have a chance to realize what's happening and stop me. The memories have been attacking me since she made the connection. It makes sense. He wouldn't want me because he forced himself on me and took my innocence long before they handed Ivy over. So many nights I lay there staring at the wall, waiting to see if he would come in. So many nights of sleep lost when he would climb on top of me and...

No. I can't think about that now. I need to find him. I need to make him pay not only for me but for Ivy. I don't know everything that happened to her, but she's gone now, and it's because of him, his actions and my parents'. I already made them pay. He's the last on the list. I don't realize tears are streaming down my cheeks until I pull to a stop a block away from his house. After wiping my face clear with the back of my hand, I climb into the back of the van to find the bag where AK stows our weapons.

It's in the back corner, strapped to the wall. I unravel the strap and pull it down to dig through it. I tap the flashlight on my phone to see inside. Digging around, I find a few blades and a gun which I pull out. Something grabs my attention, though. It's not a weapon. I pull out the thick six-by-nine rectangular, flimsy block to see a fucking romance novel. *Finding Each Other* by Sara Hurst. What in the actual fuck? How am I in love with this man?

I put the book away, and when I climb back up front, I can see his house at the end of the block. Muling over my options,

I decide it's best to drive up and hope the spare key is under the pot by the door. Once I'm parked in front of the house, I turn the engine off and put the key in my pocket. I take a deep, steadying breath before I exit the van and head up the walk. The torment of memories from a past life invades my thoughts as I reach the door. Carefully, I decide to check if the door is unlocked. Somehow, I get lucky, and as soon as I twist the knob, the door opens with a quiet creak. I freeze, waiting for someone to come barreling down the stairs. After a moment, when nothing happens, I decide to take a step inside and close the heavy wooden barrier to the outside world behind me.

Taking guarded steps up the stairs, one by one, I finally reach the landing. I look around the open concept living and dining room, where so many holidays were spent. My stomach turns at the things that have happened under this roof. A loud creak gives away that someone else is here with me. I quickly sneak to the left, finding myself in a dark hallway. It's then that I see him step out from the kitchen with a glass of bourbon in his hand. He takes a seat in the armchair across from the large picture window and sips on his drink.

"Come on out, Chloe. I know you're here." His voice is as thick with smoke damage as I remember.

I step out from my hiding place, the gun raised in my hands aimed directly at his head. Crossing the room in a quick fluid motion, I come face to face with the man who abused me for most of my childhood. The man who is responsible for my sister's abduction and eventually her death.

"It's been a long time, Uncle," I sneer. "Abduct anyone else's sister recently?"

"Oh, Chloe, don't be like that. You know you were my favorite. I just couldn't risk someone wanting to buy you when you weren't pure like Ivy was, or like Echo." He chuckles as if it's a joke, and I don't understand the punchline. "When no one wanted either of them, I was stuck with them. Instead of letting them go, I just used them when I was around or had my boys take care of them for me."

"Are you out of your fucking mind? You raped them, left them to their own devices in a room that was all but a torture chamber." I growl. "Do you know what they did to them? How they killed Ivy?" I scream at him.

"Aww, sweetheart. Don't be like that. It wasn't personal."

My vision darkening as I lock my gaze on him. The man who took so much from so many people. Not just Ivy and Echo, not even me. All the others who he abducted over the years. It sickens me.

"How many?" I find myself unable to stop from asking. I close the distance and sit on the coffee table before him. The barrel of the gun still aimed at him, only now, instead of his head, it's aimed at his chest.

He cocks a brow. "Why does it matter, Chloe?" Shaking his head as if my question is absurd. "It's not going to change the past or the future. There will always be someone I'll be able to buy and sell."

His admission has fire rushing through my veins.

*I'm going to take pleasure in ending this motherfucker.*

"Please, fuck, oh my god!" I scream at the top of my lungs. "Pocket, please!"

He's been edging me for what feels like forever. All I hear is AK's heavy breaths and grunts behind me. He feels so fucking good.

"Bear, I don't care if she's in charge. If you don't let me come, I'm going to stab you in the nuts as soon as I can walk." I sob, a mixture of pain and pleasure.

He chuckles darkly as he leans down and whispers into my ear, "I love it when you're feisty, Sunshine."

With that, I feel his arm snake around my torso and slide down my stomach to between my thighs. His cock throbbing inside me, making the piercings provide even more stimulation. He presses hard against my clit, and I see stars. With one more thrust, I feel him empty himself inside me, an orgasm coming over me that lasts for several long moments. The room is filled with expletives as we find our release together. I collapse onto the bed, my face buried into the pillows.

"Fuck. You. Angel." I groan each word, sure to enunciate.

"Shit!" AK roars, startling me straight out of my post-orgasmic haze.

"What? What happened?" I pop up so quickly it's almost cinematic. Looking around the room, I realize Pocket is nowhere in sight. "Oh, god," I cry.

I race out to the living room, glancing around the open space only to find that AK and I are the only ones in the apartment. She wouldn't, not like this.

"Sunshine, go get dressed. We need to go, now!" He growls as he goes to the hall closet and pulls out a large bag.

I turn back and race to the bedroom and pull on the first pair of yoga pants I can find. They're pink and floral; Pocket hates them. I tug a black sports bra over my head before slipping into a pair of socks and black sneakers. AK is back in the room with me, dressing quickly in black jeans and a black Henley, the black leather work boots finishing off the look. He just fucked me into submission. I shouldn't be getting turned on again.

He crosses the room in two long strides, pressing his lips against mine with a chaste kiss. "Let's go get our girl."

I follow him out to the living room where he grabs a backpack from the couch and lifts it onto one shoulder. We head out the front door and race down the stairs.

"Fuck, Pocket!" he shouts. "Baby, I'm gonna need you to do something you're not going to want to do."

I nod at him. "I trust you, Bear." I offer a weak smile as he takes my hand and drags me across the parking lot to where a beautiful motorcycle sits. He hands me the backpack, and I put it on, snapping it across my chest, so it doesn't budge.

"I won't let anything happen to you." His declaration as he tosses a leg over to straddle the bike warms my heart, and he extends his hand to help me on. "I've got you."

I climb on behind him, clinging to him. "Ok, spider monkey," AK attempts to joke.

"Just call me Bella," I murmur behind him.

"Hold on tight." Is the last thing I hear before we're off.

The drive to Pocket's uncle's house has my stomach twisting in knots. I haven't been to this neighborhood in years. Glancing around and taking in the familiar surroundings only lights a determination inside me. We have to get her. I can't let him hurt her the way he hurt us. It takes only a few minutes once we get through the front gate to find his house with the van parked out front. I see Pocket's bright blue hair through the large picture window facing the street. She's sitting with her back to the front of the house. She's leaving herself vulnerable like this.

"We need to get inside," I shout at AK as soon as he brings the bike to a stop.

I jump off behind him, stumbling slightly before finding my footing.

"Sunshine, take a second to stretch. You're not used to being on a bike and with what we were doing before." His words die when I glare at him. "Ok, or we can just rush in, guns blazing."

"I don't care for the sarcasm. You don't know what he's capable of, Bear," I snap at him.

"I know I don't, but I need to get the weapons from the bag before we rush in. I told you before, I will end anyone who threatens either of you." He smirks at me. "I thrive in situations like this, Sunshine."

He disappears behind me, and I feel tugging and pulling on the backpack. He hands me a knife over my shoulder, knowing that's what I'm most comfortable using. After a few more moments, he must have finished emptying the contents because he turns me around and unhooks the bag, letting it drop behind me.

"Let's go." He takes off for the front door.

I don't bother responding, just stalk behind him like a shadow. When we reach the front door, he tries the knob, which is unlocked. Light from inside the residence peeks through as he pushes the door open. With his gun raised in front of him, we slink through the opening, careful to not make a sound. Startling either of them could be dangerous for everyone.

"You think the things you've done to me, to all the people you've taken, all the harm, trauma, and death that has come to the people you have ever had your hands on. You really think it's 'no big deal'." I hear the pain in her rushed words.

"Really, you're a little old for tantrums, don't you think, Tink?" Johnny's response has me pushing on AK and attempting to get to her. He holds his arm out, not letting me pass, and frustration builds inside me. I need to know she's ok.

"A little immature of you to give yourself a name like Johnny Hymen," Pocket says her sarcastic tone with a bite to it. "Harris didn't have the same ring to it, I guess, when you can be so on the nose, you fucking psycho."

"Considering you filled one of my men with gasoline and blew his head off with fireworks," he pauses, gesturing between them. "Pot, Kettle."

"Actually, that was my girl. She had quite a bit of pent-up rage from what you caused." The pride in her tone makes my heart ache.

AK takes a step forward, testing the stairs. He cautiously waves for me to follow him. Staying only a beat behind him, when we finally get to the top of the steps, AK has his gun pointed in the direction that Pocket and Johnny are seated.

"I didn't expect her to get on the bike." Pocket sighs in defeat.

I heard the bike as soon as it approached; I knew it was only a matter of time before they would come inside. Ignoring the telltale creak of the door, I continue my tongue lashing of this motherfucker. Not long after, I see AK out of the corner of my eye, Echo following closely behind him. Pride fills me, seeing her here, knowing she conquered one of her fears and got on that bike.

"Killer." AK's voice is sharp with a building frustration. "You should have waited for us. You've left yourself open to too much fucking potential backlash."

"I really don't give a shit. He's caused so much pain. The things he did to me. He's the reason that Echo has been through so much, the reason I—Iv—" I stutter, choking on her name, unable to say it.

I see a glint of joy in Uncle Johnny's eyes at my pain. Unable to control my temper, I stand, jamming my foot into his groin. A pain-filled scream fills the room, which brings me so much joy. He's cupping his dick, hunched over in pain when Echo pokes her head out from behind AK who looks like he's seen a ghost.

"He's the reason she's gone, yes." Echo's voice is stronger than I've heard it since I've had her back in my life. I stiffen at how casual and direct she makes the statement. Acknowledging my sister's death.

"Ech," I try to interrupt but she puts her hand up, motioning for me to let her continue.

"So many people have been taken, killed, or worse, because of him." She takes a tentative step closer. "But, Angel, facing him alone isn't going to help you find closure. He did these things to me, too. Let me be here with you."

I barely nod when she takes a step closer, not quite ready to see him as closely as I am. Uncle Johnny raises his gaze to us, his eyes so dark it's like a switch has been flipped. I've seen it before. But I'm not the scared little girl I used to be. My concern is for Echo. I turn my head to see her, so proud that she's standing straight with her shoulders back, ready to fight. The way her jade eyes sparkle in defiance, she will not be controlled by this man. Not anymore.

Her eyes go wide, and half a second before I'm caged in powerful arms, an overwhelming smoky scent fills my nostrils. I struggle against him, trying to get away, knowing it's a waste. He won't let me go. As strong as I've become over the years, this is one position I never expected to find myself in.

"You motherfucker, if you don't let her go right the fuck now." AK's voice is full of venom. I know he'll strike the second he has a chance.

"Actually, I think we can make a deal for your precious Chloe." Johnny sounds so smug it sickens me.

I don't miss the surprise in AK's eyes when he hears my birth name. He hides it well enough from Johnny that he doesn't catch it. That's all we need, him to think he has one over on us.

"Unfortunately for you, I don't make deals with your kind of predator." He stalks closer, but Johnny lifts one of my knives he snatched from my waistband to my neck, pressing it into my flesh. For the first time in years, I'm terrified of a blade being used on me like this.

"Uh, uh, uh," Johnny scolds, "One step closer, and I will slit her throat before you lay a finger on me."

Echo's face is red as she stands in the background watching everything unfold. "Little Spark, close your eyes. It's ok, you don't need to watch this." I try to soothe her from my compromised position.

I see a fire in her eyes, she looks almost giddy. Like she was when we killed Chris.

"What's the deal, Johnny?" she snaps the question.

"Simple, I get you back. They can leave unscathed." I hear the smile in his voice.

"Absolutely fucking not," AK barks, full of fury.

"Deal," Echo announces. "But I have a few conditions."

"I don't think you're in a position to make any type of demands," Johnny replies from behind me, annoyed at her attempt to negotiate.

"Actually. I think I am." She takes a step closer. "See, I've spent twelve fucking years at your disposal. Twelve years of you using me, abusing me, allowing others to do the same if not worse. Did you know James would cut us every single time? That Chris would force himself into our asses without any type of lube, and then be furious at us when we were bleeding after and unable to walk?"

She pauses, waiting for a response that doesn't come.

"I'm sure you knew. You made it your business to know everything that they did to us. But here's the thing, Johnny." She takes a breath before continuing, "I will not allow you to hurt me or anyone else I love again, you psychotic motherfucker, understand?"

She doesn't give him a chance to respond this time; she reaches behind her back and pulls out one of AK's handguns. Raising it to eye level, she squeezes the trigger. I'm jolted backward to land on top of Johnny. Scrambling to get away when I hit the floor, I stand to see blood pooling at the back of his head. The entry wound on his forehead.

"How the fuck?" I look at Echo, pride filling my chest.

"AK had me practice for a bit the day we went out for supplies." She shrugs nonchalantly.

"You nearly gave me a fucking heart attack," AK groans as he closes the distance between us. He grips my chin, staring into my eyes. "Are you ok?"

I shake my head. "No. But I will be."

Turning to face Echo, he does the same to her, forcing her to look into his eyes. "And you, Sunshine?"

"I'm fantastic. Can I set him on fire now?" She bounces on her toes.

AK and I both share a look and start laughing.

"Yep, Little Spark is so appropriate." I can't help but shake my head at her.

"Are you really going to skim over the fact that she admitted she loves you?" I question Pocket as we load my bike into the van.

"Can we talk about it at home? I want to see fire." Echo's mind set on the task at hand.

Pocket's eyes light up with humor as she climbs into the van. Echo opens the passenger side door and perches herself on the seat, staring at me expectantly. I chuckle as I put the gas can back in the van. Closing the doors, I race to the bottom of the stairs just inside the house, striking a match and dropping it before I take off for the driver seat. I feel a gust of heat behind me as the house is engulfed in flames.

The drive back to the apartment is quiet. Neither of them quite ready to say anything, and I'm exhausted after the fuck fest Pocket pushed us into. I feel like I'm going to sleep for a month.

"So, you know the payback for what you did is going to be a bitch, right?" Echo announces from the front seat as if she's reading my mind.

"What did I do?" Pocket's attempt at innocence is comical.

"I'm curious if we can have you tearing apart your drywall." I smirk at the memory she once shared with me.

"Fuck me," she groans.

"We will," Echo chimes in, in song.

"No more musical episodes for either of you," I admonish with a chuckle.

By the time we reach the apartment, we're all exhausted. After a very quick shower, the three of us collapse into bed. Pocket sandwiched between me and Echo. Reaching my arm across the bed, I hold on to them both. The rise and fall of their chests lulling me into sleep.

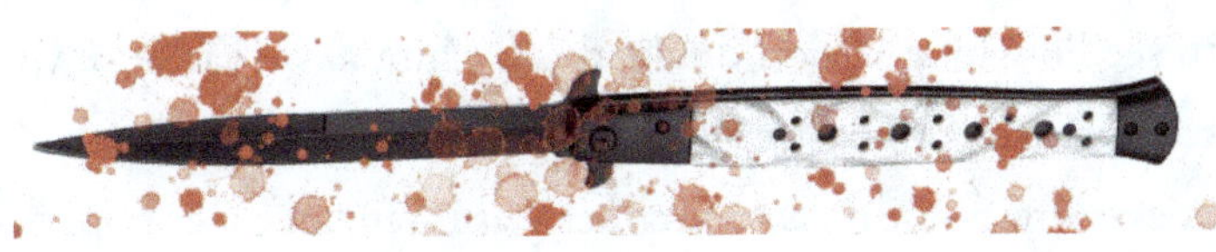

A loud crash pulls me from my slumber. I leap from the bed and take in my surroundings. I'm still half-conscious. When I realize there's sun coming in from the windows, I wipe the sleep from my eyes and slowly step toward the noise.

"Don't you dare, Chloe. You will not blame yourself for this shit," Echo yells.

I guess I'm going to have to share my name now. Ugh.

"If I hadn't blocked it out, I could have found you both sooner, Ech! I could have saved you both!" Pocket screams back at her.

"Angel, no. It's been a long time," Echo admits quietly. "Hey, nothing you could have done would have changed what happened. It took both of you to get me out."

I hear Pocket's sobs as Echo closes in on her.

"No matter how much I love you, how much I believe in you, you wouldn't have been able to get us both out. They had us restrained more when it was the two of us." The defeat in her voice is telling. "Until she was gone, the only time we were left without restraints"—she chokes as she relives the memories—"was if they were having a party and wanted us upstairs to pass us around. Apart from that, at least one of us was always tied up or bound. They didn't want us strong enough to run."

"I wish you didn't kill him. I'd like to have kept him around to see how long it would take to skin him alive. I'm sure we could find a cannibal on the dark web to sell his body parts to." Pocket's response makes me chuckle as I step out to see both of them.

"How long have you been there?" Echo asks.

"Long enough," I admit.

"Ech," Pocket calls while closing what little distance was between the two of them.

"Yea?"

"I love you, too." She smiles before pressing her lips against Echo's. They get lost in one another for a while, the kiss becoming so heated, I clear my throat before they get too far gone.

"As much as I would love to join in and continue that, there's something else we need to discuss." I move to sit on the couch. "We can't stay here. We've caused too much of a scene. It's going to lead back to us, and the three of us are far too pretty to do any jail time."

"We can leave by nightfall. That will give me enough time to pack up my essentials." Pocket's response is almost robotic.

"I mean, I really only have enough for a backpack, so I just need ten minutes," Echo jokes.

"I'll go get organized. You two decide where we're headed. I'm not picky as long as I've got you two." She smirks before she heads to the bedroom.

"You know," I say as I turn to Echo who sits down next to me, leaning into my chest. "She's changed so much since you've been back."

"What do you mean?" The confusion written across her face is precious.

"Her past may have turned her into a killer, and even killed something inside her. But, Sunshine, you're the one who brought her back to life." I wrap my arms around Echo's torso and press my lips to her hair. We sit there in silence for a while, just enjoying one another's company when Pocket comes out of the bedroom, glaring at me.

"What did I do?" I ask, rolling my eyes in exasperation, sitting Echo and I up straight from our relaxed position.

"Why did I not know you read romance books?" She holds up *Finding Our Way* by Sara Hurst. "This is the second novel by this author I've found in your shit. What gives?"

"First off, I told you. I have sisters. Kat and her friends love Sara's books, so I told her I'd read them." I chuckle. "Besides, I'm man enough to admit that Jackson Murphy Holt is the ultimate book boyfriend." I relax back into the couch, pulling Echo back into my chest.

Echo giggles in my arms. "I love you."

"I'm sorry, can you repeat that?" I ask, sitting up again.

"You heard me, Bear." She turns her face to me, pressing her lips to my cheek before laying back against me.

Well, I'll be goddamned.

A month later

We've been sitting in this room for a week. My face has been buried in my screen for four straight days, constantly looking for a way we can get this guy alone. Apparently, a hired hit-person's job description isn't just 'get in, shed blood, and get out'. It's also about finding a weakness to cause the least amount of unintentional bloodshed. I must admit, it's much less fun doing it this way.

I let out a heavy sigh as I bring up another set of surveillance feeds I recently hacked. People really think that their wireless security cameras are helping keep us out, meanwhile, I'm over here finding new ways I can skin this motherfucker alive with just things he has in his living room.

The sudden sound of skin pounding against something has me perking up. I stand, leaving my spot to find my loves.

"If you two are fucking without me again, I'm going to be pissed." I groan as I tear my top off over my head only to find Echo punching AK's target covered palm.

"What the fuck?" I ask as I start to pull my shirt back on.

"I thought she should learn to fight." AK shrugs.

"Leave it off, Angel. I'll take care of you as soon as I take him down," Echo chimes in from in front of AK.

A sly smirk pulls at my lips as I lean against the door frame watching the two of them. AK has his eyes on me, and Echo takes the opening, bending her knees and sweeping his leg out from under him. He lands on his back with a loud thud. She climbs on top of him, straddling his waist.

"I told you, Augustus Kensington, I would get you where I wanted you." She chuckles, bending down to press her lips to his, grinding her hips against his groin.

"Fuck, Sunshine. I thought we agreed you weren't going to use my government name," he groans as she changes direction. "You're both insatiable."

"Yea, but you love us," Echo and I respond in unison, her ignoring the comment about not using his name. I know she's going to tease him with it occasionally, and it's going to lead to her ass being the most beautiful shade of red. I can't wait.

She's been doing so well over the last month, knowing that there is no one coming for her. She's flourishing, and I couldn't be prouder. Even if they had tied me down for a full forty-eight hours and held me on the brink of insanity before they let me come as payback for my little escape. It was torture. I fucking loved it.

I cross the room and kneel next to her. Her answering grin tells me it's about to get interesting. She's been toying with control a bit more since we left my apartment and have been traveling for hits. This is the first time that she gets to pull the trigger since Johnny. She's got some pent-up adrenaline coursing through her veins, which apparently, we get to take advantage of.

My computer dings from the other room with a facial recognition notification. The target in question is home. I frown apologetically, and she lets out a whimper.

"No fair."

"We'll take care of you later, Sunshine." AK thrusts up into her, startling her enough that she loses her balance and tumbles off of him.

"I hate you both," she groans before she helps AK up, and they follow me as I walk to my laptop.

The target is sitting at his desk with a bourbon in hand. I roll my eyes at his choice of drink. It's the third time he's done this at the same time this week. I think we've found our weakness.

"We can sneak in before and spike the drink. It's been the same every day," I announce confidently.

"Once he's out, Sunshine can go in and light the place up," AK agrees, wrapping a powerful hand around the back of my neck. I melt into him. I can't fucking stand what he does to me.

"Yay!" Echo cheers with so much enthusiasm it's startling.

"My Little Spark, such a pyro." I snort.

We spend the next few hours talking through the plan and mapping it out. It's a hell of a lot easier when it's just me I have to look out for, though, I wouldn't change how we operate for anything. They make me better in so many ways, and the sex is just out of this world.

My story may have started out with the worst kind of trauma, but now I live my life with love by my side. My days are filled with taking down the worst kind of human beings imaginable, and I get paid for it. I don't think it's all that bad after all.

My family, your support during this journey has been incredible.

To my Stupid Face Moron, ditto.

My alpha team, you are the MVP and I can't imagine this journey without you.

Sara - My boo. I'll forever be thankful that you slid into my DM's. You are phenomenal, and I love you!

K.D. - My ride or die, I love you and I'm so freaking proud of you!

To the friends who have helped me through the difficulties with completing this book. The tears shed and constantly bringing me back, reminding me I am not too much. Thank you. There will never be enough words to express the gratitude I feel towards you.

To my Mono-Moose Patreon subscribers; Claudine, Cheryl & Jennifer.

To the FBI Agent who tracks my search history, I'm even more curious about your reaction to this one.

Lastly, but most definitely not least, my readers. Your love, support, and encouragement means so much and I can't wait to share even more stories with you all!

Additional titles by L. Clara

Firework - Prequel  MM (Joel and Lance's story) coming 2025

Endgame


The Unexpected Series

*The Unexpected Match*

The Unexpected First

The Unexpected Reunion

The Unexpected Third – MFF

The Unexpected Dance – Coming late 2025

Smalltown

Pumpkin Spice and Mr. Right

Mafia

Ludovico's Vengeance

Stand Alone - Dark Romance

KILLER IN OUR POCKET

Endgame

**The Unexpected Series**

The Unexpected Match

The Unexpected First

The Unexpected Reunion

The Unexpected Third

The Unexpected Dance (Coming late 2025)

**Mafia Books**

Ludovico's Vengeance

**Dark Romance**

Killer In Our Pocket

**Smalltown**

**Pumpkin Spice and Mr. Right**

# ABOUT THE AUTHOR

I'm an introvert. Well, until you get to know me. Then I won't shut up. I'm married to my ride or die; he's the doctor to my Clara. (IYKYK). We have a little boy who is growing way too fast and is already way too smart for my own sanity. I've had an unhealthy obsession with *Gilmore Girls* and *Buffy the Vampire Slayer* for years. You'll see the references throughout my writing. I've loved reading for as long as I can remember, but physical books with traditional novel paper give me the ick! So, you'll find me reading on my Kindle or listening to audiobooks on the regular.

Click HERE to Stalk me on all social media!

www.ingramcontent.com/pod-product-compliance
Lightning Source LLC
Chambersburg PA
CBHW071107100726
47908CB00008B/2293